Hannah Parker

By Ken Walters

Dedication

To the descendants of Hannah Parker,

This book is a tribute to the life and legacy of our remarkable ancestor, Hannah Parker. In these pages, we have sought to bring to life the world she inhabited, piecing together the fragments of history to tell her story as faithfully as the evidence allows. While creative licence has shaped the fictional elements, the heart of this tale remains rooted in truth—a reflection of the trials, triumphs and tragedies that marked her life and those around her.

As her descendants, we feel a deep connection to the past and a profound respect for the strength and resilience she must have possessed. This story is not just a chronicle of her times but a testament to the enduring spirit of the family she helped to create.

With admiration and respect,

Ken and Andy Walters

Preface

"Hannah Parker" is the culmination of a journey that began with an unquenchable curiosity about our family's past, brought to life through the tireless research of Andy Walters. Building on the legacy of his parents' work, he has spent over 30 years uncovering the rich history of our ancestors. Without his meticulous efforts, this story could never have been told in such detail.

As the author, I have aimed to take that wealth of historical data and transform it into a living, breathing narrative that captures not only the essence of Hannah Parker's life but also the Victorian world she inhabited. While every effort has been made to adhere to historical facts where possible, there is inevitably a degree of creative interpretation to fill the gaps and bring characters and events to life.

This novel represents the blending of two approaches: the careful reconstruction of history and the art of storytelling. "Hannah Parker" is not just the story of one woman but of a time and place of social struggles, personal triumphs, and the unspoken sacrifices of many women like her during the Victorian era.

I owe Andy an outstanding debt of gratitude for his years of dedication to the research that underpins this book. His work has provided a strong foundation for this narrative, and his passion for our shared history shines through in every chapter.

I hope that "Hannah Parker" serves not only as a tribute to the life of one woman but also as a reminder of the countless untold stories from our past, stories that shaped the present in ways we may never fully comprehend.

Ken Walters

Contents

1842	6
Elizabeth Glenn	12
Will Parker	26
1849	41
Jimmy Kimberley	58
1858	70
Martha Griffiths	80
William Griffiths Jr. (WG)	100
Tom Green	143
John Plant	175
1898	198
Richard Griffiths	215
1901	230

1842

The year is 1842. Great Britain has a new queen—Victoria. She has been on the throne for only five years and married to her beloved Albert for two years. They already have two children—her namesake, Victoria (who will become the German Empress and Queen of Prussia as the wife of German Emperor Frederick III) and the future King of England, Edward (but he will have a long wait to be King). Her family will dominate Europe for generations to come.

With a young monarch, it is an exciting period of hope and change. Her reign will mark a revolution in all facets of society, both in the United Kingdom and the great British Empire. On that topic, after abolishing slavery in South Africa some eight years prior, the conflict between the British and the Boers in South Africa began to grow. In this year, hunter Dick King famously rode for more than ten days into a British military base in Grahamstown to warn that the Boers had besieged Durban. The British army dispatches a relief force. Later in the century, activity like this will develop into what is known as the Boer Wars. In addition, the first Anglo-Afghan war (as it will become known) ends this year. Other than this, the conflict with other nations (USA, France, etc.) experienced in recent decades is subsiding, and we are on friendlier terms with those nations. But by the end of the century, British imperialism and expansion will grow at a rate never experienced in human history—and the sun will no longer set on British territory.

Horse and carriage remains the predominant mode of travel in Great Britain. The steam train is a burgeoning form of travel. The Liverpool and Manchester Railway opened just over a decade ago and is setting the pattern for modern railways globally. Queen Victoria is the first reigning monarch to travel by train this year—and this encourages confidence in the new form of noisy, dirty but swift travel that joins communities. This decade is to be, by far, the greatest decade for railway growth—but it is still considered a risky form of transport, with many deaths reported in newspapers. Over the next couple of generations, people will travel by train more frequently as the growth in railway travel becomes more desirable. But for now, travel over distance remains with the horse and carriage—and the movement of goods on land is by horse and barge.

The general public encountered the first-ever income tax during peacetime with the introduction of the Income Tax Act: seven pence (7d) in the pound for incomes over £150. However, this will not touch the average household for many years. A bailiff or shepherd earns less than a quarter of this. It was also in this year that the Mines Act of 1842 became law. This law prohibited underground work for all women and boys under ten in the United Kingdom.

The Royal Mail—already over three hundred years old—had recently introduced the Uniform Penny Post. A component of the comprehensive reform of the Royal Mail, the postal service became more accessible to the British population by setting a charge of one penny for carriage and delivery between any two places in the United Kingdom of Great

Britain and Ireland, irrespective of distance. Like the railway, it will set the standard for the world. Although many can't read or write well, communication over distance is becoming more accessible, and communities are becoming closer and more informed.

People have also begun to witness many types of human-powered vehicles, but the bicycle, as we know it today, is still a few decades away.

In the heart of England, there is a thriving city—Coventry. Home to nearly 40,000 people, the city is on the brink of rapid growth, a trajectory that will see it more than double that figure by the end of the century. This growth and prosperity bode well for Coventry's future.

The city has a colourful past. It housed the parliament for Henry IV and Henry VI. It was home to several monastic orders severely hit by Henry VIII's dissolution of the monasteries some three hundred years prior. Monasteries, convents and other properties belonging to the orders of Carmelites, Greyfriars, Benedictines and Carthusians were either sold off or dismantled. Coventry experienced its most significant loss when its first Cathedral, St Mary's Priory and Cathedral, was largely demolished. This destruction left only ruins, making it the only English Cathedral destroyed during the dissolution. Nonetheless, the towering spires of St. Michael, Holy Trinity and Christchurch are visible from miles around at this time.

Coventry also had other royal connections at the time of the gunpowder plot in the seventeenth century. If Guy Fawkes had been successful in killing King James, the Catholic Princess Elizabeth residing at Coombe Abbey (spirited away in the night to Palace Yard, Coventry) would have been crowned Queen in St. Mary's Guildhall and pledged England's allegiance to the Pope (and Catholicism) once again.

One hundred years later, during the English Civil War, Coventry became a bastion of the rebellious Parliamentarians. Only two hundred years before this story, a Royalist force led by King Charles I attacked Coventry. However, after a two-day battle, the attackers could not breach the city walls, and the city's garrison and townspeople successfully repelled the attack, forcing the King's forces to withdraw.

During the Second Civil War, Parliamentarian Coventry held many Scottish Royalist prisoners. The idiom "sent to Coventry," meaning to ostracise someone, likely originated from this period due to the city folk's often hostile attitude towards the prisoners.

Following the restoration of the monarchy, as punishment for the support given to the Parliamentarians, King Charles II ordered that the city's walls be slighted—damaged and made useless as defences. This was carried out in 1662.

In the 1700s and early 1800s, ribbon weaving—along with watch and clock making—became Coventry's staple industry, employing around 10,000 weavers in Coventry and its surrounding towns, like Bedworth and Nuneaton, a few miles north. The resilience and innovation of these people, who turned adversity into opportunity, are truly inspiring.

The opening of the Coventry Canal in 1790 aided Coventry's growth. It gives the city a connection to the growing national canal network. During these years, Coventry became one of the three main British centres of watch and clock manufacture and ranked alongside Prescot in Lancashire and Clerkenwell in London. Samuel Vale set up his firm Vale & Sons in Coventry in 1747. Vale was among the most skilful watchmakers in the city. In 1790, Samuel Vale hired Richard Rotherham as his apprentice. Rotherham quickly emulated Vale, crafting movements with high-quality materials and incredible attention to detail. After being listed as a partner in the firm and years of hard work, in 1842, Vale & Sons was renamed 'Richard Kevitt Rotherham & Sons'. The company only grew from there—partly due to the commission of a watch by the future King Leopold I of Belgium to honour his beloved wife, Princess Charlotte. By 1899, Rotherham had over 700 employees and manufactured Coventry's famous Godiva Clock.

In a few years, Coventry will overshadow and become the main centre of British watch and clock manufacture. Approximately 2,000 people will work in the industry, including highly skilled artisans specialising in producing precision components.

The people of Coventry are an embodiment of this revolutionary history. Unafraid to challenge authority and even royalty. Defiant. Strong characters that are argumentative amongst one another but unified in their goal. Driven. Creative. Innovative. Indomitable. Newcomers to the city soon incorporate this spirit—or fail and move on. It becomes intrinsic. It has to be that way to be able to survive. In the next century, the city will lead the world in manufacturing bicycles, motorbikes, motor cars, tractors, aircraft and the jet engine—revolutionising how we grow and harvest food and travel. There will be no part of the world that the innovations of the Coventrians will not have touched.

On the outskirts of this bustling, vibrant, mediaeval city, where people live cheek-by-jowl, are green fields home to tiny hamlets and villages cut by ancient roads and paths, new rail tracks and canals—where a new generation of farming communities reside.

Elizabeth Glenn

Elizabeth was born in 1816 in Stretton-on-Dunsmore—a quiet country hamlet surrounded by farmland halfway between Coventry and Rugby on the Roman Fosse Way. It is about a nine-mile journey to the nearby city. A walk of three or more hours for farmers taking stock to market at New Gate—the entrance to the old walled city (and the route to London) where the taxes levied by the corporation did not encumber trade, and therefore unruly and ungoverned at the same time.

Her father, William Glenn, was born in the village in 1788 under the reign of the third Hanoverian monarch, George III. He was the first Hanoverian born in England and the first to use English as his first language. People widely remember George III for losing the American colonies and going mad. William lives there content with a simple country life and will continue to do so for his entire life. He is a farmer. Her mother, Elizabeth (known as Bess), was 27 when her namesake was born.

Her parents' trade was in raising and marketing animals for meat, milk, wool, and eggs, and at times and when needs must, they were involved in local crop production. Cattle, sheep, and pigs were the mainstay of the household.

Elizabeth was a quick birth. She followed Thomas in 1810 (six years older) and her sister, Hannah, in 1813 (three years older). Elizabeth was doted on by her siblings, and she doted on her younger sister, Sarah Glenn, who arrived when she was three years old in 1819.

As a young girl, she occasionally travelled to Coventry by horse and cart. She became excited by the prospect of her visits. On her approach, she crosses the bridge over the River Avon where Coventrians repelled Prince Rupert and his Royalist army during the civil war a few hundred years earlier—not once, but twice—just as the enormous spires of Christchurch, St. Michael and Holy Trinity began to dominate the horizon. Smoke rises from the newly built factories. The modern buildings are the first to observe close-ups en route. Her eyes are wide at the magnificence of the brickwork, glazing, and adornments. The spaces between them grow smaller as they continue.

Factories employing specialist workers springing up alongside workshops of individual master artisans come next. As they approach the city, tall buildings are juxtaposed with small wooden-framed ancient structures and magnificent Georgian facades with many glass-framed windows, oversized doors, and polished brass furniture visible through the gaps of black metal railings. People are bustling on their way to their business. Scruffy young boys and girls in rags. Dirty faces, hands, and legs—no shoes. Some are playing in the street with a simple hoop and stick. Some are begging from the more affluent, such as those working at the watch and ribbon weaving factories. The smart gentlemen in their frock coats fitted along the torso and flared at the waist, ending roughly around the knees. People fashionably wear trousers in a straight cut. A leather or gold chain fastens a gold watch to the waistcoat buttonhole. A small pocket conceals the watch, designed specifically for this purpose. People retrieve it occasionally to remind themselves of its wealth and status. And the women in their large, full conical skirts bellowed by crinolines, hoops, and petticoats. The distinctive large 'leg of mutton' or gigot sleeves with a narrow, low waist, achieved through a combination of corsetry to restrict the waist and full sleeves and skirts that made the waist appear smaller by comparison. Bonnets. Bonnets with wide semicircular brims framing the face for streetwear—heavily decorated with trim, ribbons, and feathers.

Married women were distinct. They wear a simple linen or cotton cap for daywear, trimmed with lace, ribbon, and frills, and tied under the chin—fineries—long earrings, a necklace, a bracelet. Hands covered by lace gloves. But most wear a simple shawl over their heads—a sign of poverty. Elizabeth has a glimpse of her future. She yearns to be the woman in the large house, the beautiful dress, with the man on her arm who is gutter side and who will treat her as such. She plans to move to the city when she is old enough and climb to the seemingly unassailable heights of grandeur.

As years went by, her experience and love for the nearby city grew to accompany her father on every occasion she could. She was excited to be part of the vibrant, exciting, and comparatively intense space—far away from the quiet fields and animals of farm life. Her brother does not feel the same. He will farm the land like their father had. After the sales at New Gate, they will venture into the city, passing the old Whitefriars Monastery, now converted to a workhouse where inmates worked twelve hours a day in winter and thirteen during the summer, with only half an hour for breakfast and an hour set aside for lunch. The workhouse school provided young children with a basic education, their saving grace. They enjoy a meal at an inn. If there are enough coins, it will be at her father's favourite inn—The Golden Cross. Formerly the Coventry Mint. It is located on the corner of Pepper Lane and Hay Lane, at the heart of the city and is the hostel for working people. They serve locally brewed beer from Tower Street. They serve cold meat, fresh bread, and butter. Simple food. Opposite the inn is Bayley Lane. Originally, the castle's perimeter and where the courtrooms are now situated. There is the occasional scuffle by people with unhappy outcomes. On the opposite corner is the towering spire of St. Mary's, and across the street is the Guildhall. Until recently, the Guildhall had served as the city's armoury and as its treasury but was now the headquarters for administration for the city council. Many finely dressed Coventrians walked these streets, creating a lasting impression on the impressionable young Elizabeth Glenn.

Elizabeth beamed, thinking, "Father, may we visit the market after the sales?" Elizabeth asked, her eyes sparkling with anticipation as they passed the imposing facade of the old Whitefriars Monastery.

"Aye, if we finish in good time," William replied, a gentle smile playing on his lips as he tousled her hair. "We'll stroll through the market and perhaps treat ourselves to a meal at The Golden Cross."

Elizabeth's face lit up with joy. Her mind was already racing with thoughts of the colourful stalls, the aroma of freshly baked bread, and the city's lively atmosphere.

"Oh, Father, you always know how to make the day feel like an adventure," she exclaimed, her excitement barely contained. "I can't wait to see what treasures we might find at the market!"

William chuckled at his daughter's enthusiasm, feeling warm at the prospect of sharing this simple pleasure with her. "I'm glad you're looking forward to it, my dear. Exploring the market with you by my side is always a delight." As they continued, the promise of the market visit added an extra spring to their steps, filling their afternoon with bright anticipation racing with thoughts of the bustling city and its vibrant life.

As the cathedral bells chimed in the afternoon, it signalled time to return to the ostler to collect their ride and begin the horse and cart journey home. William Glenn will stop by the Coventry Herald and Observer newspaper in Pepper Lane and read the recent news bulletins in the windows. If enough coins were in his pocket, he would buy a newspaper to enjoy by candlelight back in Stretton. He is only slightly educated—but can read enough to look at the copy posted in the establishment's window. The old lady sitting on a stool with a rickety table afore will cry out to the passersby that she is selling the most recent daily publication with an almost incomprehensible bellow.

"Father, can we get a newspaper today?" Elizabeth asked, her eyes lighting up with anticipation.

William smiled at his daughter and replied, "If there's enough left after our meal, my dear, we shall definitely get a newspaper. I know how much you enjoy me reading it to you."

Elizabeth beamed with joy, and they continued walking, discussing the articles they hoped to find in the newspaper.

The journey back to Stretton will be sad for Elizabeth. She pines for the city and the life she dreams it can provide, which is far away from country life. Crossing Toll Bar Bridge again, she will peer over her shoulder at the city.

"Why do you always look back at the city, Lizzie?" Thomas asked, noticing her wistful gaze.

"I dream of living there someday," Elizabeth confessed. "I want to be one of those fine ladies in beautiful dresses, walking arm in arm with a gentleman."

"You'll find your way, Lizzie," Thomas said, though his heart belonged to the farm.

In 1832, at the tender age of sixteen, Elizabeth stood before her father, Will, in their modest farmhouse kitchen. The late afternoon sun filtered through the windows, casting a warm glow on her determined face. Elizabeth had spent weeks rehearsing this moment in her mind, gathering the courage to voice her dreams.

"Father," she began, her voice steady despite her racing heart, "I wish to speak with you about my future."

Will, a sturdy man with weathered hands and kind eyes, set down his mug of tea and gave his daughter his full attention. "What's on your mind, Lizzie?"

Elizabeth took a deep breath. "I wish to live in the city and work as a silk weaver," she said, her eyes shining with determination.

Will's brow furrowed, concern etching lines across his forehead. "The city? Are you certain, Elizabeth? It can be a harsh place, full of dangers and temptations. Why would you want to leave our peaceful farm?"

Elizabeth stepped closer, her hands clasped tightly in front of her. "I am certain, Father. I've given it much thought. The farm is beautiful, and I love our life here, but I yearn for more. In the city, I can learn a trade, better myself, and perhaps even make a name for our family."

Will leaned back in his chair, studying his daughter. "And why silk weaving, of all trades?"

Elizabeth's expression softened. "I've always been drawn to intricate work that requires patience and skill. When I visit the city and see the silk shawls—how fine and delicate they are—I know what I want to do. I want to create something like that. Something beautiful, crafted with care and precision. The artistry of silk weaving calls to me, Father, not just the idea of a trade."

Will stood up and walked to the window, gazing at the fields he had tended all his life. "It's not an easy life, Lizzie. The hours are long, the work is demanding, and the city... well, it's a far cry from what you're used to."

Elizabeth joined him at the window. "I know it won't be easy, Father. But I'm ready for the challenge. I want to grow, learn, and see more of the world than our fields."

Will turned to face his daughter, seeing not just the child he had raised but the woman she was becoming. He saw her mother's spirit in her eyes, that same yearning for something more.

After a long moment, Will sighed and gently touched Elizabeth's shoulder. "Your mother would be proud of your ambition, Lizzie. She always said you had a fire in you."

Elizabeth's eyes widened with hope. "Does this mean...?"

Will nodded slowly. "It means I'll help you fulfil your dreams, even if it somewhat breaks my farmer's heart. You're right—there's a whole world beyond our fields, and you deserve the chance to find your place in it."

Tears of joy welled up in Elizabeth's eyes as she threw her arms around her father. "Thank you, Father! I promise I'll make you proud."

Will hugged her tightly, his voice gruff with emotion. "You already have, my dear. You already have."

As they stood there, embracing in the warm kitchen, both father and daughter knew that a new chapter in their lives would begin—one filled with challenges, opportunities, and the promise of a brighter future.

After some deliberation, William Glenn arranged suitable lodgings and found a trustworthy tradesman for his daughter. Life will change forever. She appears to be bettering herself with a contemporary trade that will serve her well; the chance to find a gentleman who will be the head of her family—but all the while, she is drawn to the excitement of the city. It's inns with their music, dancing, beer, wine, and spirits—and the men and women that frequent such places. The farm life is long behind her.

The Golden Cross Inn quickly became Elizabeth's second home with its timber-framed walls and bustling atmosphere. Situated at the corner of Hay Lane and Pepper Lane, it was a lively crossroads for travellers, merchants, and townsfolk alike. The clatter of mugs, the murmur of conversation, and the hearty laughter filled the air as Elizabeth worked shifts as a barmaid. The work was demanding, but she thrived on the energy of the place, grateful for the extra income and the chance to connect with people from all walks of life.

As the weeks passed, Elizabeth became more attuned to the rhythms of the inn, moving effortlessly between tables, greeting regulars, and sharing a friendly word with newcomers. Her quick wit and warm smile endeared her to the patrons, earning her generous tips and the respect of her fellow workers. Among them were a few kind souls who took her under their wing, teaching her the unspoken rules of the inn and the ways of the city.

One crisp evening, after a bustling night, Elizabeth was surrounded by her new friends at one of the corner tables. The flickering glow of the lanterns cast a warm light over the group, their faces flushed with the cheer of drink and camaraderie. Her closest companions included Mary, a sharp-tongued but good-hearted woman who had worked at the Golden Cross for years, and her new beau, Charlie Smith, a cheerful young man who handled the deliveries.

"Here's to new beginnings," Elizabeth declared, lifting her glass. Her eyes gleam with a blend of resolve and excitement for the first time since leaving her family's farm.

"To your future, Lizzie," her friends echoed, clinking their glasses together in a loud, joyful toast. "May the city be kind to you, and may your hands weave both silk and success!"

Elizabeth took a sip, savouring the rich taste of ale and the warmth of the moment. The inn buzzed with life around them—a fiddler played a lively tune by the hearth while a group of travellers swapped tales of faraway lands. Elizabeth smiled, knowing she was at the beginning of something significant.

"You'll do well, Lizzie," Mary said, giving her a playful nudge. "The city's not always kind, but you've got more spirit than most. Just keep that fire in your heart and a bit of caution in your step."

Charlie grinned and leaned in. "And don't forget, we're here for you. We've all seen how hard you work and how quickly you've made your mark. Here's to a bright future!"

As the night wore on, toasts and laughter flowed freely, sealing the bonds of friendship. Elizabeth found herself imagining what lay ahead—the skills she would master, the independence she would earn, and the life she would build. In those moments, surrounded by new friends in the golden glow of the inn, she felt more confident than ever that her decision to leave the farm had been right.

The Golden Cross would come to hold a special place in her heart, not just as a place of work but as a symbol of her growing confidence and resilience. There, amidst the laughter and stories of her companions, Elizabeth began to feel genuinely at home in the city. Over time, she would become wise to its ways, learning to navigate the bustling streets and the social intricacies that defined city life.

Each day, Elizabeth mused, she might be one of those elegant women she had once envied—poised, self-assured, and accomplished. She pictured herself draped in fine silks, walking with an air of quiet confidence through the city's bustling streets. But for now, she was content to raise her glass and toast to her journey, knowing that her dreams were no longer distant fantasies but steadily taking shape with each passing day. Her growing circle of acquaintances made the days fly by, and the lively evenings gave her a sense of belonging in this vast, unpredictable city.

One such evening, Charlie burst through the door of the Golden Cross Inn with a wide grin. A regular presence, Charlie was a wiry lad with an infectious energy that seemed to light up any room he entered. He waved to Elizabeth across the busy tavern as he threaded through the crowded tables.

"Evenin', Lizzie!" Charlie called out, his voice carrying above the din. "I've got someone I want you to meet!"

Curious, Elizabeth looked up from the tray she was balancing. Charlie rarely introduced anyone with such enthusiasm. As he approached, she noticed a tall, broad-shouldered young man following him, his face partly shadowed beneath a worn cap.

"This here's Will Parker," Charlie said, clapping a hand on the newcomer's shoulder. "He's a mate of mine. Figured he could do with a good drink and a bit of cheer after a long day's work."

Will tipped his cap politely, offering Elizabeth a reserved smile. "Pleasure to meet you, Miss," he said in a low, steady voice that hinted at humility and strength. Up close, Elizabeth could see that he had kind eyes, though there was a guardedness about him, as if life had taught him to be wary.

"Pleasure's mine, Will," Elizabeth replied warmly. "Any friend of Charlie's is welcome here. Take a seat—first drink's on me."

The three of them settled into a table near the hearth, where the crackling fire cast flickering shadows on the walls. As the evening unfolded, Elizabeth learned more about Will. He had grown up in the city. He had ambitions of building a family business in silk weaving. It was hard work, but he had a steady determination that impressed Elizabeth.

Charlie, always eager to keep spirits high, leaned in with a grin. "Will's one of the strongest lads you'll ever meet, Lizzie. Saved me more than once from trouble, he has."

Will shrugged modestly. "Just look out for mates, that's all."

Elizabeth could see why Charlie held Will in such high regard. Beneath his rough exterior, Will seemed honest and dependable, rare and precious qualities in a place as unpredictable as the city.

As the night wore on and the inn grew quieter, Elizabeth felt more at ease in their company. She realised that the friendships she built were not just a distraction from her ambitions but an essential part of her growth. With all its noise and clamour, the city was a place where she was learning to stand on her own—but it was also where she was finding connections that made her stronger.

By the end of the evening, Will had relaxed a little, and Elizabeth found herself enjoying the easy banter that had sprung up between them. When it was time for them to leave, she offered a genuine smile. "You're welcome back anytime, Will. The Golden Cross is always better with good company."

"Thank you, Miss," Will replied, a hint of warmth in his voice as he tipped his cap again. "I'll be back, for sure."

As Charlie and Will entered the cool night air, Elizabeth watched them go with a sense of satisfaction. Her world was expanding in terms of her dreams and the people she was coming to know and trust.

The city was still vast and mysterious but no longer lonely. With every toast and every new friendship, Elizabeth felt herself growing closer to the poised, confident woman she aspired to be—a woman not just of ambition but of genuine connections rooted in trust and shared hopes.

Will Parker

Will was born in 1811 in Radford, one of the small hamlets on the city's fringe that its relentless growth would soon engulf. Will, the son of John and Amelia Parker, came from a line of weavers who laboured diligently at their looms from home. His childhood was woven into the rhythm of the loom's steady clatter, with his earliest memories filled with the sights and sounds of silk being transformed under the hands of his parents. By the age of twelve, his own hands had learned to guide the threads, shaping his ambitions.

As Will grew into his teens, the boy who had once worked alongside his parents at the loom began to transform into a young man of quiet determination. His hands, once small and untrained, now moved with the deft precision of a seasoned weaver. The hum of the looms became a familiar soundtrack to his daily life, their rhythmic clatter echoing the steady growth of his ambition. But the ever-increasing clamour of city life, the vibrant, bustling streets of the nearby city began to call to him with promises of opportunities beyond the confines of his family's humble home. With each passing year, Will's aspirations expanded beyond the mere goal of maintaining the family trade; he envisioned building a weaving business of his own, a dream that drove him to work harder and dream bigger. His youthful exuberance gave way to a more thoughtful, contemplative demeanour. Still, his eyes retained their spark of youthful enthusiasm, reflecting the hopes he harboured for a future beyond the loom's incessant rhythm.

Will's days of hard work were often followed by nights in the city's lively inns, where the air was thick with the smell of ale and the sound of laughter. In one of these warm, bustling taverns—the Golden Cross—he first laid eyes on Elizabeth Glenn. She was 19, with a wild, untamed spirit that intrigued and captivated him. Elizabeth, who occasionally worked at the inn, had a presence that demanded attention, her laughter bright and her gaze sharp.

"Good evening, Miss Glenn," Will greeted her one night, tipping his hat with a grin that hinted at something more than mere politeness. His voice was smooth, wrapping around her like the warm embrace of a winter's fire.

"Good evening, Mr. Parker," Elizabeth replied, her eyes alight with a mischievous sparkle. Her cheeks, still flushed from the inn's warmth, glowed softly in the flickering candlelight. "What lures you to the Golden Cross this night? The ale or something more?"

"Ah, perhaps it's not the ale that's drawn me here, but rather the company," he teased, his voice light but layered with a sincerity that made her smile.

Elizabeth laughed, a sound so joyous it seemed to push back the shadows of the dimly lit room. Her defences, carefully maintained around most, began to crumble in the face of Will's charm. Their banter, at first playful, soon deepened, thickening the air with a tension neither could ignore.

After a few shared drinks and countless exchanged glances, they slipped out into the cool night. The streets around them were quiet, and the city's usual bustle was muted under the cover of darkness.

"Catch me if you can, Will!" Elizabeth called out, her voice a teasing lilt that danced on the cool night air as she darted into a narrow alleyway. Her skirts billowed around her like a swirling mist, the fabric whispering against her legs as she moved with an enticing grace.

Will grinned, his heart pounding not just from the chase but from the heady thrill of the evening. "And when I do, Miss Glenn," he replied, his tone rich with playful challenge, "you'll owe me more than just a dance. Perhaps a secret or two?"

Elizabeth glanced back over her shoulder, her eyes gleaming with mischief and something more profound, like promise. "Oh, you think so, do you? And what if I told you I might have a secret worth more than a dance?" Her voice was a sultry murmur, full of seductive allure.

Will's laughter echoed through the empty alleyway as he quickened his pace. "I do believe I might take you up on that, Miss Glenn."

Their playful chase wove through the shadowy streets, their laughter mingling with the night's stillness until they reached the secluded grounds of St. Michael's Church. Under the canopy of the starlit sky and the solemn gaze of ancient stone saints, their mirth softened into a more intense, electric anticipation. The air was thick with a charged silence as Will finally caught up with Elizabeth, his hands gripping her waist with a mix of urgency and tenderness.

"Elizabeth," Will breathed, his voice husky with desire as he pulled her close. The space between them was charged, each breath mingling with the next, a prelude to the inevitable.

Her eyes met his, dark and deep, as she whispered, "Will, I want…"

The words dissolved as their lips met in a kiss that was more than just a meeting of mouths—an exploration, an ignition of all the passion and longing building between them. The kiss was fierce and consuming, like a storm breaking over a tranquil sea. It was a declaration of the emotions they had harboured secretly, finally laid bare under the cover of darkness.

Their bodies pressed together, skin against skin, the cool night air mixing with their heat. The world beyond the churchyard faded into insignificance as they gave themselves over to the moment, their movements fluid and eager, driven by a raw, unrestrained longing. The ancient stones of the church stood as silent witnesses to their union, a sacred ground that bore the weight of their passion.

As their ardour subsided, they lay together on the soft grass, their breaths mingling in the cool night air. The stars above seemed to shine brighter, the world outside their intimate cocoon falling away into a distant murmur. They lay entwined, feeling an exalted sense of completion and joy. They found a new, profound connection, their hearts swelling with bliss that transcended the physical—a shared secret that made the night an eternal promise.

In the spring of 1836, beneath the very spires that had once borne witness to their clandestine passion, Elizabeth and Will stood before the altar of St. Michael's Church, hands clasped and hearts entwined. The vows they exchanged were not just of love but of duty – sealed by the new life Elizabeth carried within her, a testament to the night their fates had been forever bound. The families are present. Her sister, Hannah, bears witness along with Charlie Smith—the best man.

"Do you, Elizabeth Glenn, take this man, William Parker, to be your lawfully wedded husband?" the vicar asked, his voice resonating through the sacred space.

"I do," Elizabeth replied, her voice steady and clear, though her heart raced with the promise of a new life.

"And do you, William Parker, take this woman, Elizabeth Glenn, to be your lawfully wedded wife?"

"I do," Will answered, his eyes locked on Elizabeth's, filled with a blend of love and determination.

The birth of their first child was a joyful crescendo to the night of passion that had ignited their love. Richard was born into the world on a crisp morning, his arrival marked by a symphony of triumph and relief. His cry was solid and clear, a testament to his vitality and the deep bond he shared with his parents. The tiny hands that gripped Elizabeth's finger seemed to promise a future filled with hope and joy. As he grew, he became the embodiment of their love—a living reminder of their stolen moment beneath the stars.

Five years later, after troubled pregnancies, Thomas arrived, and his birth was a swift and welcome addition to their growing family. He was a bright-eyed child, and his arrival was greeted with exuberant joy that seemed to double the warmth in their home. For a brief while, it seemed as though their little family was complete, each child a testament to their love and devotion.

But the harsh reality of the times struck cruelly when Samuel was born. From the beginning, it was clear that he was frail and delicate. Despite the tender care of his parents and the constant vigilance of the family, the harsh winter took its toll on the tiny, fragile life. Like a candle flickering in a tempest, Samuel could not withstand the cold and illness that accompanied the season.

Samuel's small form grew ever weaker as the snow fell thick and silent outside. Elizabeth's heart was shattered as she watched her infant struggle, each breath more laboured than the last. The winter seemed endless; a cold expanse mirrored their home's growing chill.

When Samuel passed, the house was heavy with the weight of their grief. The little cot, once a symbol of hope, now stood empty and forlorn. Elizabeth clutched a small, worn blanket to her chest, her shoulders shaking with sobs that came from the very depths of her soul. Her tears fell freely, mingling with the sorrowful silence that enveloped them.

"Why did this happen, Will?" Elizabeth's voice was a fragile whisper, the pain of her loss palpable in every word. She sank to her knees beside Samuel's empty cradle, the small blanket a futile comfort in her trembling hands.

Will knelt beside her, his own grief etched deeply into his features. He gathered her into his arms, his heart aching as he felt her pain. "We must trust in God's plan, my love," he murmured, his voice a low, comforting balm against the raw edge of their sorrow. "Samuel is at peace now."

Elizabeth buried her face in his chest, her sobs muffled by the strong, steady heartbeat she had come to rely on for solace. Will's embrace was both a refuge and a promise, a reminder that even in their darkest hour, their love and their surviving children would be their guiding light.

As they mourned their lost son, the memory of Samuel remained a bittersweet echo in their lives, a reminder of the fragility of their joys and the strength of their love. Each day, as the seasons changed and their family continued to grow, they would remember Samuel with a tender, lingering sorrow, honouring his brief presence in their lives with quiet reverence.

In 1841, as the chill of winter crept over the city of Coventry, Will Parker reached his thirtieth year. His home, a modest yet newly built cottage on Tower Street, stood proud on higher ground near the remnants of the old Cook Street gate. The area, a rising prospect for the future, was a sanctuary from the floods that besieged the lower city during winter. Here, amidst the gradual encroachment of urban sprawl, Will toiled diligently as a ribbon weaver six days a week, his efforts fuelled by a steadfast determination to forge a prosperous future for his family.

One evening, after a long day at the loom, Will retired to their modest yet prestigious home. The night was settling in, casting a soft glow over the city below. Elizabeth, his wife of seven years, was busy setting the table for supper, her movements a dance of practised efficiency.

"How was your day at the loom, Will?" Elizabeth enquired, her voice crisp with the warmth of routine as she adjusted the placement of the plates.

"Long and tiring but fruitful," Will responded, his voice tinged with the weariness of a hard day's work. He sank heavily into a chair, his fingers stretching and curling as if to shake off the day's labour.

"And yours, my dear?" he asked, his gaze softening as he watched her.

"Busy with the children and the house, as always," Elizabeth replied, her voice carrying a note of frustration. Her dreams of a more opulent life seemed increasingly distant as she moved about their simple but respectable cottage.

Elizabeth, at twenty-five, found herself grappling with a gnawing dissatisfaction. The reality of her daily life was a far cry from the grand visions she had once cherished as a young girl, stepping into the bustling city with her father's guiding hand.

That evening, as twilight deepened and the city lights began to twinkle like stars below them, Elizabeth looked out of the window, her expression distant and contemplative. The candlelight flickered softly against her face, casting shadows that danced with her unspoken dreams.

"Will," she began softly, her voice wistful. "Do you ever think of what might have been?"

Startled by the melancholy in her voice, Will looked up from his meal. "What do you mean, Elizabeth?" he asked, his brow furrowing with concern.

Elizabeth turned to him, her eyes reflecting the dim light, a hint of sadness clouding her features. "The dreams I had as a girl, of living in grandeur and not merely surviving," she said, her voice a mere whisper. "I imagined a life of elegance and refinement, not just this simple existence."

Will sighed deeply, his heart aching for her unfulfilled dreams. He reached across the table, taking her hand in his, his grip firm yet tender. "Elizabeth, my love, I understand the dreams you once held close to your heart," he said softly, his voice imbued with both compassion and determination. "I work tirelessly, hoping that one day, our efforts will bring us closer to those dreams."

Elizabeth's eyes glistened with unshed tears as she looked at him, her grip tightening around his hand. "I know you do, Will," she said, her voice quivering slightly. "It's just that sometimes, I feel as though those dreams are slipping further away, buried beneath the weight of our daily struggles."

Will squeezed her hand reassuringly. "We shall not give up, Elizabeth," he said, his voice firm with conviction. "I may not have the means to give you all you desire just yet, but I promise you this: I will strive every day to build a future where those dreams can one day flourish."

Elizabeth nodded, her heart warmed by his resolve. "Thank you, Will," she said, a faint smile breaking through her melancholy. "It means more to me than you know."

As they shared their evening meal, the flickering candlelight seemed to cast a gentle glow over their renewed hope. Though their dreams remained just out of reach, the strength of their love and determination to build a better life provided a light that guided them through the darkest of nights.

The following year, as the seasons turned from the bite of winter to the softness of spring, Elizabeth Parker's dreams continued to flicker like a distant star, elusive and just out of reach. The gnawing ache of unmet aspirations had begun to cast a shadow over her days, seeping into the very fabric of their household. Though Will worked tirelessly, his hands roughened by the constant toil at the loom, Elizabeth's yearning for a life of greater elegance and comfort remained unfulfilled. The pressures of their modest existence weighed heavily upon her, her discontent manifesting in small, sharp remarks and a lingering sadness that coloured the corners of their home.

Richard, now seven, and young Tom, just two, were the bright spots in her life, their laughter and energy providing fleeting moments of solace. Yet, with each passing day, the strain of her unspoken frustrations added a subtle tension to their interactions, making the simple act of maintaining their home feel more like a Herculean task.

One crisp morning, as the dawn light filtered through the small windows of their Tower Street cottage, Elizabeth sat in the nursery, her thoughts a whirlpool of hope and despair. The arrival of their fourth child was imminent, a new life that might bring a fresh breath of hope or deepen the burdens she felt.

As the labour pains came, Elizabeth's resolve was tested, yet her love for her family remained unwavering. Will, ever the diligent and loving husband, stayed by her side, his own face etched with worry and fatigue. The room was filled with hushed murmurs of encouragement and the occasional soft cries of pain from Elizabeth, a poignant reminder of the sacrifices she made for her family.

Finally, amidst the hushed reverence of their shared anticipation, the baby's first cries pierced the air. Elizabeth, though exhausted, cradled the newborn with a tenderness that belied her weariness. "Welcome to the world, little Hannah," she whispered, her voice catching with emotion as she held the child close, her heart momentarily lighter as she looked into the tiny, scrunched-up face.

Standing by her side, Will couldn't help but be moved by the sight. "She is as beautiful as her mother," he said, his eyes shining with tender pride. His voice was gentle, his love for his wife and their new daughter palpable in the warmth of his gaze. "Hannah Parker has arrived, and she is perfect."

Elizabeth managed a weary smile, her eyes wet with tears of both joy and lingering sadness. "Thank you, Will," she said, her voice barely more than a whisper. "She is our blessing, isn't she?"

Will nodded, taking Elizabeth's hand and squeezing it gently, the touch a silent vow of support. "She is. And she will bring us more joy than we can imagine," he assured her, though he, too, felt the weight of their reality.

As the days passed and the newness of Hannah's presence began to settle into their lives, the family adjusted to the addition with a mixture of hope and continued struggle. Elizabeth's resentment didn't vanish overnight, but the sight of her children and the unwavering support of her husband provided moments of reprieve from her discontent. Will continued his labour with an unshakable determination to provide for his family, his love for Elizabeth and their children a beacon in the murky waters of their daily lives.

Elizabeth's dreams of grandeur remained in the background, but Hannah's presence and the promise of future days offered a glimmer of hope, a reminder that sometimes the greatest joys can come from the most modest of lives.

Four years after Hannah's arrival, the Parker household welcomed another daughter into their lives. Elizabeth Parker, now nearly resigned to the reality of her unfulfilled dreams, found herself at a crossroads of emotions—pride and weariness blending in the small, tender moments of her daily life. The new baby, whom they named Lizzy, brought with her a fresh wave of affection and, for a moment, the promise of something new.

In the nursery, Elizabeth carefully lifted Lizzy from the cradle, her hands gentle as she settled the infant into the crook of her arm. Her eyes, though weary, softened as she looked down at the tiny face. Ever the supportive husband, Will stood nearby, his expression a mixture of love and fatigue. He had long since accepted their modest life, though he still cherished the moments of familial closeness.

"Look, Hannah," Elizabeth said, her voice a delicate whisper, as she guided her elder daughter towards the cradle. "This is your new sister, Lizzy."

Hannah, now a bright and inquisitive four-year-old, approached with a sense of awe. Her small hands clasped together in anticipation as she peered at the new arrival. "She is so tiny, Mama," Hannah said softly, her eyes wide with wonder. The innocence of her gaze starkly contrasted with the tangled emotions Elizabeth felt inside.

Elizabeth's tender smile carried an undertone of melancholy as she brushed a tear from her cheek. "She will grow, just as you have," she said, her voice catching slightly. "And we will love her as much as we love you."

Sensing the weight of the moment, Will stepped closer, placing a reassuring hand on Elizabeth's shoulder. "She's a beautiful addition to our family," he said, his voice warm and steady. "I'm sure she'll bring us much joy."

Elizabeth nodded, her gaze lingering on Lizzy's peaceful face. Yet beneath the surface of her smile lay a quiet resignation. "I hope so," she replied softly, her words more to herself than to Will. "She's so small now, but she'll grow. We all grow, don't we?"

Hannah looked up at her mother, sensing a shift in the atmosphere. "Mama, will Lizzy be as big as me one day?"

Elizabeth's heart ached at the innocence in her daughter's voice. "Yes, darling. With time, she'll grow up just like you," she answered, though her thoughts wandered to the dreams she had once harboured.

Noting the distance in Elizabeth's eyes, Will tried to bridge the gap. "And we'll do everything we can to give her and all our children the best life possible," he said, his tone firm but gentle.

Elizabeth managed a wan smile, her heart heavy with the weight of unspoken longings. "Yes, Will. We will. For their sake and our own, we'll try to make the best of what we have."

As she settled Lizzy back into the cradle and turned to tend to Hannah's curious questions, Elizabeth couldn't shake the feeling of dreams deferred, the shadows of her ambitions flickering faintly in the background of her everyday life. She took comfort in the love she had for her family, though it was a bittersweet solace that did little to ease the quiet ache of what might have been.

The nursery, with its soft light and the gentle cooing of a new baby, was a world of small comforts, but for Elizabeth, it was also a reminder of the dreams that had dimmed with each passing year. She held on to the hope that perhaps, in nurturing her children, she might find a fragment of the future she had once envisioned, even if it was not the grand life she had imagined for herself.

1849

In the mid-19th century, the landscape of Victorian England was transformed by the rapid expansion of the railways, a feat of engineering and ambition that stitched the country together in a web of iron tracks. Among the many men who laboured to bring this revolution to life was Thomas Ball, a man whose life was as turbulent as the times in which he lived.

Thomas had started his working life as a silk weaver, his hands once deftly working the looms in the dimly lit rooms of Nuneaton. But as the railways began their relentless march across the land, promising speed, connectivity, and a new kind of progress, Thomas was drawn to the allure of this modern wonder. He traded his shuttle for a shovel, becoming a railway labourer on the Trent Valley line. This was no ordinary line; it was a direct artery from London to the North West of England and Scotland, bypassing the older, more circuitous route through Birmingham. The Trent Valley line, opened in 1847, cut through the heart of the Midlands, threading its way through towns and cities like Stafford, Lichfield, and Rugby, giving rise to new opportunities and hardships.

Thomas and his wife, Mary, made their home in Nuneaton, a town bustling with the energy of industrial growth. Though modest, their cottage was within earshot of the clattering trains that had become the region's lifeblood. Yet, despite the external signs of progress, their marriage was anything but a story of shared prosperity. The railways brought not only work but also long hours, meagre wages, and a rough camaraderie among the men who built them—a camaraderie that often led Thomas into the arms of temptation.

"Where have you been, Thomas?" Mary would ask, her voice tinged with both weariness and resignation, as he staggered through the door late at night, the smell of ale and cheap perfume clinging to him like a second skin.

"Out," he'd reply gruffly, his eyes avoiding hers as he slumped into a chair. "Work's been hard today. Need a drink to take the edge off."

"And the women, Thomas?" Mary pressed, her voice breaking. "Are they also part of your work?"

Thomas would scowl, his temper rising as quickly as the flush in his cheeks. "Mind your tongue, woman," he'd snap, though there was little real menace in his voice, just the weary anger of a man who had lost his way. "You've no right to question me after the day I've had."

But the truth of it weighed heavy on Mary, more so with each passing year. Their marriage, once a source of hope, had become a vessel of sorrow. The tragedies they had endured together—the six babies lost in their short time as husband and wife—had carved deep lines into Mary's face and heart, leaving her a shadow of the girl she once was.

"Why, God?" she would whisper to herself in the quiet of the night, her hands resting on her empty womb. "Why take my babes from me? What have I done to deserve this?"

Thomas, though he grieved too, sought solace in the bottle and in the company of other women, trying to drown the pain that seemed to follow him wherever he went. His temper, always quick to flare, often spilt over into violence, leaving Mary bruised in body and spirit. With its long hours and brutal work, the railway became both his escape and his prison—a place where he could lose himself, if only temporarily, in the rhythm of the tracks and the camaraderie of his fellow labourers.

But no amount of work, drink, or womanising could fill the void left by the losses they had suffered. Thomas would return home late, the night air biting at his cheeks, only to find Mary sitting by the hearth, her eyes hollow and distant.

"Thomas," she'd say softly, almost as if speaking to herself. "We can't go on like this. We're tearing each other apart."

"And what do you suggest, Mary?" Thomas would ask, his voice tinged with bitterness. "What's left for us after everything?"

"We could start again," she'd reply, though her words lacked conviction. "Maybe…maybe away from here. Away from the railways and the memories."

But they both knew it was an empty hope. The railways had bound them to Nuneaton just as surely as they had bound the towns and cities of England together. And though they dreamed of escape, of a life free from the shadows of their past, the reality was that they were trapped—trapped by circumstance, grief, and the choices they had made.

The years passed, and with them, Thomas and Mary grew more distant. Their marriage was a fragile thing held together by little more than routine and the shared weight of their sorrows. Thomas continued his work on the railways, his back bent under the strain of labour, his nights spent in taverns and other women's beds. Mary, meanwhile, stayed at home, tending to the small garden that provided their only solace, her heart hardened by years of disappointment.

Yet, despite everything, a part of her hoped that one day, Thomas would return to her, both in body and spirit. That one day, they might find a way to heal the wounds that had festered between them.

But that day never came. The railways continued to expand, and with them, Thomas's absences grew longer, his return visits more bitter. Mary, left alone in their cottage, could only watch as the trains thundered by, carrying her husband further away from her with each passing day.

One drizzly autumn morning, as the mist curled around the cobbled streets of Nuneaton like tendrils of some unseen spectre, Mary Ball pulled her shawl tighter around her thin shoulders and set off toward the town's high street. Her steps were deliberate, her mind turning over thoughts as dark as the clouds that hung low in the sky. The wind whispered secrets to her as she walked, the weight of years of sorrow bearing heavily on her heart.

Mary had long considered herself a good wife—dutiful and patient—enduring Thomas's infidelities and the bruises left behind by his volatile temper. But the years had chipped away at her resolve, her dreams dissolving like mist in the morning sun. The losses of her babies had left her hollowed out, and with each day that passed, the hope she clung to slipped further from her grasp. Lately, a grim thought had been gnawing at her, one she could no longer ignore.

It was late in the afternoon when she reached Illife's chemist's shop on Market Place. A small, dimly lit establishment wedged between the butcher's and the baker's. The bell above the door tinkled softly as she entered, and the familiar smell of medicinal herbs and liniments enveloped her like a stale embrace. The chemist, Mr. Gilbert, a thin, balding man with spectacles perched on the end of his nose, looked up from behind the counter, his eyes narrowing slightly as he recognised Mary.

"Good afternoon, Mrs. Ball," he greeted, his voice polite but distant. "What brings you here today?"

Mary hesitated for only a moment, the lie already forming on her tongue. "Good afternoon, Mr. Gilbert," she replied, forcing a small smile. "I've got a terrible rat problem at home. Nasty creatures—they've been getting into the pantry, spoiling the food. I need something to deal with them once and for all."

Mr. Gilbert nodded knowingly, though a flicker of something—perhaps suspicion, perhaps pity—passed over his face. "Ah, yes, rats can be a real menace, especially this time of year. Are you looking for something strong, then?"

"Yes, something strong," Mary confirmed, her voice steady though her heart pounded in her chest. "I've tried everything else, and nothing seems to work."

The chemist turned and began to rummage through a shelf behind the counter. After a moment, he produced a small, white paper packet and placed it gently on the counter between them. The packet, folded tightly at the edges, held within it a quantity of arsenic crystals that sparkled faintly in the dim light.

"Arsenic," he said, his voice dropping to a near whisper, as though the very word might summon something malevolent. "These crystals are potent. Only a small amount is needed—enough to mix with a bit of food to entice the rats. But be careful, Mrs. Ball; arsenic is deadly. Keep it well away from anything you don't want harmed."

Mary stared at the packet, the crystals inside glinting like the shards of her shattered dreams. "Thank you, Mr. Gilbert," she said quietly, reaching into her purse for the few coins she had brought with her.

The chemist handed her the packet, his eyes meeting hers for a brief moment as if searching for something hidden in their depths. "Remember," he warned gently, "this is not to be used lightly. Make sure it's placed where only the rats will find it."

"I will," Mary replied, her voice barely above a whisper as she tucked the packet into her bag. She offered a weak smile, but it did not reach her eyes. "I'll be careful", she said.

As she left the shop, the bell above the door tinkled again, its cheerful sound at odds with the heaviness that settled over her like a shroud. Outside, the mist had thickened, and the street lamps began to flicker to life, casting long, eerie shadows across the wet cobblestones.

Mary walked home in silence, the packet of arsenic rustling softly against the other items in her bag with each step. The world around her seemed to blur, the familiar sights of Nuneaton fading into obscurity as her mind turned over the possibilities of what she could do next.

Once home, she placed the packet on the kitchen table, staring at it with a mixture of dread and determination. The house was quiet, the only sound the soft ticking of the clock on the mantelpiece, counting down the moments of her troubled resolve.

"Just for the rats," she whispered, though the words felt hollow in her ears. The arsenic crystals lay before her, a deadly solution to the pests that plagued her—both those that skittered in the walls and the one who slept in next to her.

Mary deliberated on her purchase, her thoughts swirling with uncertainty and dread. Its presence was a stark reminder of the decision she now faced, a decision that weighed heavily on her heart.

She paced the room, glancing at the packet as if it might offer her some counsel, some reassurance that what she contemplated was justifiable. The house was quiet, save for the soft creaking of the floorboards beneath her feet and the distant murmur of the wind outside. The stillness only amplified the turmoil within her.

Finally, with trembling hands, Mary picked up the packet, its weight feeling as if it had grown with the gravity of her thoughts. She walked slowly to the mantlepiece, her movements deliberate, almost hesitant, as if she hoped that each step might lead her to a different conclusion. The dim light in the room cast long shadows that twisted and curled around her, the very walls seeming to watch her with bated breath.

As she reached the mantle, she paused, her eyes lingering on the small family trinkets that lined its surface—each one a token of a life that once held so much promise, now tarnished by hardship and despair. With a deep, shuddering sigh, she placed the packet beside the clock, its plain white paper standing out against the polished wood.

The steady tick-tock of the clock echoed through the room, each second marking the passage of time, the approach of a moment that could not be undone. The arsenic lay there, silent and still, yet charged with the weight of unspoken intentions, a presence both innocent and ominous in the flickering firelight. Though not yet made, the decision loomed over her, casting a shadow that seemed to stretch into the very corners of her soul.

It was three months later after Thomas had returned from a long day of fishing, that the fateful moment arrived. He staggered through the door, his face pale and drawn, clutching his stomach with one hand.

"Mary," he groaned, his voice thick with pain. "I feel a right mess. Must've caught something foul at the river."

Mary looked up from her mending, her heart pounding in her chest. She forced herself to remain calm, her voice even as she replied, "Perhaps some salts will help, Thomas. There's a packet on the shelf, just by the clock. Take a good dose, it'll settle your stomach."

Thomas, trusting and desperate for relief, reached for the packet. He tore it open, unaware of the deadly contents, and poured a measure into a cup of water. Mary watched, her breath caught in her throat, as he downed the mixture in one gulp.

Within minutes, the effect was horrifying. Thomas doubled over in agony, his cries echoing through the small cottage. He writhed on the floor, his body convulsing as the poison took hold. Mary stood by, frozen with a mix of dread and resolve, her eyes wide as she watched her husband suffer the fate she had so coldly orchestrated.

By the time the sun had set, Thomas Ball was dead—his life cruelly cut short at the age of twenty-eight. The grim news spread quickly through Nuneaton, and it wasn't long before suspicion turned to Mary. Whispers filled the air, neighbours casting wary glances her way, the story of the "salts" on the shelf weaving its way into the fabric of local gossip.

Authorities soon arrived, and Mary was arrested, her fate sealed as surely as the packet of arsenic had sealed Thomas's. She was sent to Coventry Assizes to stand trial, her name now synonymous with treachery and death, the mantle shelf forever marked as the place where a man's life was so callously undone.

Throughout the trial, Mary steadfastly denied any intent to murder her husband. Her face remained impassive, her voice unwavering as she protested her innocence before the judge and jury. But the weight of her crime, like the arsenic she had administered, gnawed at her conscience. It was only after the relentless ministrations of a particularly fervent prison chaplain, who gripped her hand in the dim glow of a candle and spoke with vivid urgency of the horrors awaiting her soul in the afterlife, that Mary's resolve crumbled. She confessed quietly to the prison governor, her voice trembling with the burden of her guilt.

"I knew," she began, her words halting and heavy, "I knew at the time they were not salts, but I thought... I thought if Tom had taken it himself, I should not get into any scrape about it. People would think he took it by mistake, and I would be free of blame."

When pressed to explain why she had committed such a grievous act, Mary's composure finally broke. Tears streamed down her face as she sobbed, her voice choked with the anguish of years of suffering. "My husband... he was in the habit of going with other women. He treated me so cruelly—no one knows what I have endured, the pain and the humiliation. I could bear it no longer..."

On August 9, 1849, the roads leading into Coventry were choked with an estimated 20,000 people, all eager to witness the execution of Mary Ball, the daughter of a Nuneaton innkeeper. The crowd swarmed like ants, filling every available space, their faces alight with a mix of anticipation and morbid curiosity. The execution, scheduled for ten O'Clock in the morning, was to take place at the old jail and courthouse on Cuckoo Lane, just a few yards from the Golden Cross Inn—a place where, ironically, moments of life's fleeting pleasures had once been shared over ale and hearty laughter.

As the hour drew near, the atmosphere grew increasingly charged, a strange blend of festivity and foreboding that hung heavy in the air. The gallows, stark and foreboding against the grey morning sky, loomed over the crowd like a dark omen, the final destination of a woman whose tragic story had captivated the public.

And so, as the clock struck ten on that fateful morning, Mary Ball was led to the gallows. The public execution became a grim spectacle, a macabre event that drew people from all around, turning the hanging into a grotesque holiday. Little did the onlookers know that they were witnessing the last public execution in Coventry, a final chapter in a dark era of English justice.

Mary's father, who ran the White Hart Inn where Thomas had sometimes worked, stood among the crowd, his face etched with sorrow. He had lost not only a son-in-law but now his daughter as well, a victim of desperation and the unforgiving hand of fate.

As the noose tightened around her neck and the trapdoor swung open, Mary Ball's life ended, leaving behind a cautionary tale of the dangers of despair and the tragic consequences of a life lived in suffering. The crowds slowly dispersed, the weight of what they had witnessed settling over them like a shroud, as Coventry closed the chapter on its last public hanging.

Amidst the teeming sea of over 20,000 people, Will Parker stood in the dense, oppressive crowd that had gathered for the hanging of Mary Ball. The air was thick with a mixture of anticipation and morbid curiosity, as if the very essence of human suffering had drawn these spectators from every corner of the region. The execution was a few yards from the place forever etched in Will's memory as the site where his own love story with Elizabeth had first ignited.

The morning had been grey and foreboding, and as the hour approached, the crowd's restless murmur grew into a low, anxious hum. The gallows, stark and unyielding, loomed over the gathered masses, casting a long shadow that seemed to darken the very heart of Coventry. Will's gaze was fixed upon the grim stage of the execution, the noose hanging ominously, its dark presence a cruel reminder of the tragic fate that awaited Mary Ball.

As the noose was tightened around Mary's neck, the chill of the moment seemed to pierce through Will's own heart. His thoughts churned with sorrow and confusion. The image of Thomas Ball—a man broken by his own vices, whose life had been marred by drinking, womanising, and violence—seemed to haunt him. Thomas's troubled existence and the violent end he had met now served as a mirror, reflecting back the precarious balance of Will's own life.

He thought of Elizabeth, who stood beside him, her face drawn and pale, her eyes reflecting the gravity of the occasion. He thought of their children—Richard, Tom, Hannah, and little Lizzy—and the fragile equilibrium that held their lives together. The public spectacle of Mary Ball's execution forced Will to confront the dark spectre of failure that loomed over his own marriage. The stark reality of what had transpired—the loss, the despair, and the ultimate tragedy—struck him with a profound sense of urgency.

"I will not let anger or neglect tarnish what we have," Will vowed silently, his eyes never wavering from the grim proceedings. The scene before him was a visceral reminder of the devastating consequences of a fractured relationship. He clenched his fists, feeling the cold resolve settle within him, determined to safeguard his own family from the shadows that had claimed Mary Ball and Thomas.

As the trapdoor fell and Mary Ball's life was abruptly ended, the crowd fell into a subdued silence, a collective exhalation of relief mixed with the haunting echo of what had been witnessed. Will stood amidst the dispersing throng, feeling the weight of the day's events press heavily upon him. The lesson of Mary Ball's tragic end was etched into his soul—a stark reminder of the fine line between harmony and discord, and the dire consequences of allowing that balance to falter. The finality of the hanging had not only concluded a chapter in Coventry's history but had also marked a turning point for Will, a solemn pledge to protect the love and stability he held dear against the encroaching shadows of despair and discord.

In the year 1851, Will Parker relocated his family to a modest new home on Radford Road, a shift that seemed to promise improvement yet fell short of the dreams that Elizabeth had once harboured. The bustling city of Coventry, with its burgeoning watchmaking industry, was a world that seemed to pass Will by as he clung to his old trade of ribbon weaving. The strains of their marriage, once manageable, grew more palpable, creating rifts between the couple that deepened with each passing day.

One evening, as the flickering light of a single candle cast shadows upon their small dining room, Elizabeth's frustration reached a boiling point. The clatter of the evening meal was forgotten as she confronted Will, her voice laced with desperation.

"Will," she said, her eyes blazing with a mix of determination and hurt, "the watchmaking trade is where the future lies. Coventry is transforming before our eyes. You could seize this opportunity and make a better life for us."

Will, his hands still covered in the fine dust of his weaving trade, looked up with a furrowed brow. "Elizabeth," he replied, his voice carrying a note of weary finality, "my trade is weaving. It's what I know; it's what I am. The loom is my life's work. I cannot simply abandon it for something that is foreign to me."

"But we are drowning in debt, Will!" Elizabeth's voice rose, tinged with frustration. "My dreams of grandeur—those were for our betterment, for the children's future! Yet here we are, stuck in a rut."

Their children, Richard, now fourteen, Tom, aged eleven, Hannah at eight, and little Lizzy, just five, watched in sombre silence as their parents' arguments grew more frequent. The contrast between Elizabeth's yearning for opulence and Will's adherence to tradition created a chasm that left the family feeling increasingly adrift.

One particularly heated argument erupted late into the evening, their voices echoing through the narrow confines of their home.

"Why must you always dream of more?" Will's voice was strained, the edge of his frustration cutting through the dimly lit room.

"Because we deserve more, Will!" Elizabeth's voice cracked, her tears mingling with the harshness of her words. "The children deserve more than this stagnant existence!"

Despite numerous attempts at reconciliation, their marriage was in disrepair by the summer of 1857. The city buzzed with excitement when Charles Dickens visited the Rotherham watchmaking factory, a testament to the city's rising prominence. Yet, Elizabeth, consumed by jealousy and bitterness, was absent from the festivities. She could not bear to be among the wives of the prosperous watchmakers, her own unfulfilled dreams casting a shadow over her spirit.

Will, weary from the constant discord, left the family home. His absence adding to Elizabeth's growing isolation. Now turned forty, Elizabeth found herself alone, her dreams of a grand life slipping further away. Richard, now a successful watchmaker in his own right, resided at a prestigious address on Earl Street, providing her with occasional financial support despite her known indiscretions with younger men who visited her.

Sensing the decline of his mother's circumstances, Richard contemplated leaving Coventry to seek success elsewhere. Elizabeth's remaining children, Tom, Hannah, and Lizzy, were her sole companions as they lived in modest lodgings at Chauntry Place, near the river and Swanswell Gate.

Meanwhile, Will resided on Greyfriars Lane, near Ford's Hospital, his heart heavy with the weight of a life and love he had endeavoured to sustain but ultimately could not preserve.

The tension and strife that had marked their years together now seemed to hover like a spectre over their separate lives, leaving both Will and Elizabeth to reflect on the dreams they had once shared and the lives they now led apart.

Jimmy Kimberley

In the heart of 19th-century Coventry, nestled among the winding streets and modest homes, the Kimberley family made their dwelling at 2 Court, 12 Cox Street. The family, consisting of Joe Kimberley, a hardworking head of the family, his wife Cathy, and their two sons, Jimmy and the younger Torsend, lived a life marked by simplicity and the persistent challenges of their environment. Their home, situated close to the river and a nearby pool, was often at the mercy of the elements. The river's seasonal temper brought floods to their doorstep, filling their modest abode with the cold, murky waters that threatened to wash away their few belongings. Yet, the Kimberleys met these hardships with a stubborn resilience, a steadfast hope that their fortune would one day change.

Born in the autumn of 1839, Jimmy Kimberley was a child who seemed destined for something beyond the ordinary. From the moment he could walk, his bright blue eyes and unruly dark curls caught the attention of everyone who crossed his path. Even in his early years, there was a spark about Jimmy—a vivacious energy that set him apart from other boys his age. Cathy often said that her son was born with a charm about him, a magnetism that drew people to him as surely as the river drew the tides.

As the years passed, Jimmy grew into his potential. By 1858, at the age of nineteen, he had blossomed into a handsome young man. His strong jawline, easy smile, and the natural swagger in his step made him the talk of the neighbourhood.

He was tall, with broad shoulders that spoke of the hard work he'd put in helping his father, yet there was a softness to his features that made him irresistibly appealing. The young women of Coventry couldn't help but notice him, and Jimmy, with his easy confidence, enjoyed the attention.

Life in Coventry was tough for many, but Jimmy had a way of making the mundane seem thrilling. He had a quick wit, always ready with a joke or a clever remark, and his laugh—boisterous and full of life—was contagious. He brought a sense of excitement to the otherwise monotonous days, whether it was a lively game of street football with the local lads or charming the women at the market with his stories. He had an uncanny ability to make people feel special, as if they were the only person in the world when he spoke to them.

The Parkers, who lived just a short walk away in Chauntry Place, were not immune to Jimmy's allure. Will Parker, a man of traditional values and quiet resolve, admired the young man's spirit, even if he sometimes worried about the influence Jimmy might have on his own sons. With her unfulfilled dreams and yearning for something more, Elizabeth found herself both intrigued and slightly envious of the carefree life Jimmy seemed to lead.

Even though he was a little older than Jimmy, young Richard Parker looked up to him with a mixture of admiration and aspiration. He saw in Jimmy the freedom and excitement he wished for himself, a stark contrast to the strict expectations of his own household. Hannah, still a girl but on the cusp of womanhood, would sometimes catch herself daydreaming about Jimmy's lively antics, her heart fluttering with the innocent crushes of youth.

But there was more to Jimmy than just charm and good looks. Beneath the playful exterior lay a young man with dreams of his own, dreams that reached far beyond the flood-prone streets of Coventry. He longed for adventure, for a life that didn't involve the back-breaking work his father endured. The tales of the bustling cities, of London's commerce and Manchester's factories, filled his head with possibilities. He imagined a world where his charisma could take him far from the small, damp house on Cox Street.

Yet, for all his dreams, Jimmy was still bound to the reality of his life in Coventry. He could not easily shrug off the weight of responsibility, no matter how much he wished to. His father, Joe, relied on him, especially as Torsend was still too young to take on the heavier tasks. And then there was Cathy, who looked at her eldest son with a mixture of pride and concern, knowing that one day soon, he would want more than what their humble home could offer.

The Kimberleys, like the Parkers, were a family in transition, caught between the old ways and the new world that was rapidly encroaching upon them. And at the centre of it all was Jimmy Kimberley, a young man on the brink of something greater, though even he couldn't quite see what that would be.

The stage was set for a story that would intertwine the fates of these families, their lives shaped by the choices they made, the paths they took, and the dreams they dared to chase. In the midst of it all, Jimmy Kimberley would play a role far more significant than he—or anyone else—could have ever anticipated.

Joe Kimberley, a man of formidable stature and a presence that commanded respect, worked as a blacksmith—a trade as old as time and one that required the strength of both body and spirit. His hands, roughened and scarred from years of shaping iron and steel, were a testament to the hard labour that had sustained his family through countless trials. The forge was his domain, a place where the heat of the flames danced upon his rugged face, casting shadows that mirrored the inner determination of a man who had built his life with grit and resilience.

"Ah, Jimmy, me boy, pass me the tongs," Joe would often call out, his voice carrying over the rhythmic clang of hammer on anvil. The request was simple, yet it held a more profound significance—a passing of knowledge, a subtle reminder that one day, this forge might be Jimmy's to command.

"Here you go, Father," Jimmy would reply, his own hands already bearing the early signs of strength and skill. Though still a young man, Jimmy was learning the intricacies of the craft the same way his father had before him. The bond between father and son was forged not just in blood but in the shared toil of their trade, each blow of the hammer resonating with the unspoken understanding of their legacy.

In the shadow of his older brother, young Torsend, born in 1848, he trailed eagerly, his tiny feet trying to keep pace with Jimmy's longer strides. Torsend idolised Jimmy, his admiration evident in the way he mimicked every move and every gesture. To Torsend, Jimmy was a hero—someone who could do no wrong, someone whose strength and charm he longed to emulate.

"Can I help too, Jimmy?" Torsend would often ask, his eyes wide with hope and admiration, as if helping his brother would bring him one step closer to being like him.

"Someday, Torsend," Jimmy would laugh, the sound rich and full of the easy confidence that came so naturally to him. Ruffling his younger brother's hair, he'd add, "You'll be the best blacksmith in Coventry; just you wait."

Despite the frequent floods that threatened their home, the Kimberley household was a hive of activity, brimming with the life and energy that Cathy Kimberley brought into every corner of their world. Cathy was the epitome of a nurturing mother, her love woven into the very fabric of their daily lives. She balanced the demands of their home with raising her two boys, her patience and warmth acting as a constant buffer against the hardships they faced.

Her kitchen was the heart of their home, a place where the aromas of hearty stews and freshly baked bread filled the air, wrapping the family in a comforting embrace that stood in stark contrast to the cold and damp outside. The kitchen table, worn smooth from years of use, was where they gathered—where the day's worries were left at the door, replaced by the warmth of family and the simple pleasure of a shared meal.

"Sit down, all of you," Cathy would call, her voice a melody of warmth and care. "Supper is ready, and I've made your favourite, Jimmy—beef stew with fresh bread."

There was a rhythm to their lives, one that was punctuated by the familiar rituals of work and home, of father and son, of mother and child. In the Kimberley household, even the simplest moments carried the weight of tradition, of love, of a family bound together by more than just blood. And in those moments, as the family gathered around the table, the harshness of the world outside seemed to fade away, leaving only the warmth of their shared existence, the love that held them together, and the unspoken dreams that lay just beyond the horizon.

Jimmy Kimberley was a young man of ambition, charm, and restlessness—a soul not easily confined by the narrow streets of Coventry or the predictable rhythms of life in his father's forge. While he honoured the tradition of blacksmithing that Joe had instilled in him, Jimmy's heart often strayed beyond the red glow of the forge, drawn to the allure of the unknown, the whisper of adventure that beckoned from beyond the town's borders.

Days there were spent with the clang of hammer against iron, the heat of the furnace a constant companion. Yet, even as his muscles grew strong and his hands calloused from labour,

Jimmy's mind wandered. He often sought respite from the demands of his trade at The Golden Cross, a pub steeped in history and frequented by a motley crew of travellers, merchants, and locals alike. It was here that Jimmy would sit, pint in hand, absorbing the tales of distant lands and daring exploits, his imagination set ablaze.

"Tell me more about the mountains in Scotland," Jimmy would urge, leaning in as an old traveller recounted his journeys. His eyes sparkled with a mix of wonder and longing as if, by hearing these stories, he might somehow grasp a piece of the world beyond.

The old traveller chuckled, his voice rough with age and experience. "Ah, young Jimmy," he said, patting the lad on the shoulder, "there's a world out there beyond Coventry, filled with wonders you can't even imagine. But it's not all glory—there's danger and heartbreak too."

Despite the old man's cautionary tone, Jimmy's heart was set on finding something more that would lift him out of the ordinary life that seemed to stretch before him like an endless, unchanging road. Little did he know that his destiny was not just tied to far-off places but to someone much closer to home.

Jimmy Kimberley had always felt a smouldering passion for Elizabeth Parker, a woman whose mere presence stirred something deep within him. Though Elizabeth was now 42, time had only refined her beauty, adding a depth and allure that captivated Jimmy in ways he could barely admit to himself. Yet, the close-knit nature of their community and the proximity of their families had always kept him at a distance, relegating his feelings to the realm of unspoken desire.

But within the dim, amber-lit confines of The Golden Cross, those barriers seemed to melt away. With its smoky air and low murmur of voices, the pub became a world apart from the one they knew—a place where boundaries blurred, and hidden desires could be explored. It was on one such evening, as the warmth of the fire cast flickering shadows on the walls, that Jimmy found himself once again in the presence of Elizabeth Parker.

Elizabeth entered the pub with the grace of someone who had learned to carry the weight of her years with elegance. Her striking beauty was undiminished, her presence commanding attention even in a room full of rowdy patrons. Something about her—a blend of mystery and melancholy—immediately drew Jimmy's gaze. He couldn't look away, his heart quickening at the sight of her.

As she moved through the room, the familiar faces around her seemed to fade into the background. Elizabeth was no stranger to dreams herself—dreams that had once filled her youth but had been gradually worn down by the harsh realities of life. Yet, here in the warmth of The Golden Cross, there was a spark in her eyes that spoke of those old dreams, of a life that still held untapped potential.

Jimmy felt an irresistible pull towards her, a need to bridge the gap that had always kept them apart. In this place, away from the prying eyes of their families and neighbours, he could finally allow himself to feel what he had long suppressed.

"Good evening, Elizabeth," Jimmy greeted her, his voice carrying a warmth that went beyond mere politeness.

Elizabeth turned to him, her gaze softening as she recognised the handsome young man who had always seemed just out of reach. "Jimmy," she replied, a faint smile playing on her lips. "It's been a while."

"It has," Jimmy said, taking a step closer, the familiar scent of ale and wood smoke mingling in the air. "May I buy you a drink?"

Elizabeth hesitated for a moment, a flicker of something—perhaps caution, perhaps curiosity—crossing her face. Then, with a quiet nod, she accepted. "I'd like that."

As they sat together, the noise of the pub receded, leaving them in a world of their own. They talked of many things—the changes in Coventry, the people they knew, and the lives they led. But beneath the surface of their conversation was an undercurrent of unspoken emotion, a connection that had always been there but was now finding its voice.

For Jimmy, the boundaries that had once kept him at a respectful distance from Elizabeth began to blur. In the Golden Cross, they were no longer simply neighbours or members of a community bound by propriety. They were two souls drawn together by a shared sense of longing, by dreams that had been deferred but not yet extinguished.

As the evening wore on, their bond deepened, fuelled by the flickering candlelight and their shared recognition of something neither could fully articulate. Jimmy knew that this moment, this connection, was rare—something that might never have happened outside the walls of The Golden Cross.

And so, in that small, crowded pub on a cool evening in Coventry, Jimmy and Elizabeth began to explore the uncharted territory of their feelings, each step bringing them closer to a future that was as uncertain as it was filled with promise.

Their connection was a spark that ignited between them, fuelled by shared longings and the undeniable pull of attraction. As the night deepened, so did their bond, and by the time they parted ways, something had shifted in both their lives—a change that neither could fully comprehend yet, but both felt in the very marrow of their bones.

Back at the Kimberley household, Jimmy's late nights at The Golden Cross did not go unnoticed. Cathy Kimberley, ever the watchful mother, observed her son's growing absences with a mix of concern and curiosity.

"Where have you been, Jimmy?" Cathy asked one evening, her brow furrowed as he stepped through the door well after dark.

"Just out at The Golden Cross, Mother," Jimmy replied, attempting to conceal the thrill that still coursed through him. "Met some interesting folks, that's all."

Joe, who had always been wary of the world beyond his forge, added his own words of caution. "Be careful, son," he warned, his voice a mix of gruffness and paternal love. "The world out there is full of temptations and troubles."

Jimmy nodded, though his thoughts were far from his father's warnings. His mind was consumed by thoughts of Elizabeth—her laughter, the way she listened to him with genuine interest, the connection that seemed to defy the ordinary. "I know, Father," he said, though his words lacked conviction. "But I can't help feeling that there's something more waiting for me."

As Jimmy navigated the increasingly complex web of his life—caught between his duties at the forge, the dreams that pulled him towards the unknown, and the burgeoning relationship with Elizabeth—he found himself at a crossroads. The path ahead was uncertain, but with each step, he felt the weight of his choices, the pull of his desires, and the intoxicating promise of what might be.

And so, Jimmy Kimberley, with the echoes of hammer and anvil in his ears and the memory of Elizabeth's smile in his heart, ventured forward into a future that was as unpredictable as it was full of possibility. The journey he was about to embark on would test the very limits of his ambition and the depths of his love, forever altering the course of his life and those entwined with it.

1858

Queen Victoria had been on the throne for twenty-one years, and the world around her was transforming swiftly and profoundly. In April, she and Prince Albert welcomed their ninth child, Princess Beatrice. Far and wide, the British Empire expanded, seizing the assets of the British East India Company. The innovation of William Herschel, who used Rajyadhar Konai's hand impression as a fingerprint signature in Bengal, marked a new era in contracts. Explorer John Hanning Speke discovered Lake Victoria, the source of the River Nile, while US President James Buchanan inaugurated the new trans-Atlantic telegraph cable by exchanging greetings with Queen Victoria. The Anglo-Japanese Treaty of Amity and Commerce was signed, heralding a new age of international relations.

Closer to home, the first General Post Office (GPO) wall-mounted post boxes appeared, revolutionising communication. Isambard Kingdom Brunel's SS Great Britain, the largest ship built to date, was launched on the River Thames, embodying industrial progress. The "Wedding March" by Felix Mendelssohn gained popularity after being played at Queen Victoria's daughter Victoria's marriage to Prince Friedrich of Prussia in St James's Palace, London. The new Royal Opera House in Covent Garden opened its doors. Meanwhile, Barbara Bodichon, Matilda Hays, Bessie Rayner Parkes, and others established The English Woman's Journal to discuss women's equality issues. Reforming educator Dorothea Beale took on her duties as Principal of Cheltenham Ladies' College, and the Court for Divorce and Matrimonial

Causes first convened, making civil divorce legally possible without parliamentary approval after implementing the Matrimonial Causes Act 1857.

In other significant developments, Lloyd's of London salvaged and hung the Lutine bell, symbolising maritime heritage. Lionel de Rothschild became the first Jewish Member of Parliament, a historic milestone. However, 'The Great Stink' of sewage from the River Thames disrupted work in the House of Commons. In Bradford, poisoned sweets tragically killed twenty-one people and poisoned over two hundred more when a supplier accidentally substituted arsenic for plaster in the sweets sold at the Bradford market.

The Linnean Society of London read papers by Charles Darwin and Alfred Russel Wallace, announcing a revolutionary theory of evolution by natural selection. In Cornwall, the Miners Association was established. Charles Dickens embarked on his first professional tour, giving readings from his works in 129 appearances across 49 towns throughout England, Scotland, and Ireland. During his tour in Coventry a year ago, Dickens visited the Rotherhams workshop and factory. This year, he received a Rotherhams gold-case pocket watch in appreciation of his support for the Coventry Institute, established in 1855 by amalgamating The Mechanics' Institution and The Religious and Useful Knowledge Society. The primary aim of The Mechanics' Institution was to promote literary and scientific pursuits among the working classes.

In 1858, Will Parker marked his forty-seventh year with a heart heavy with the weight of time and trials. He had spent his life at the loom, his hands weaving not just ribbons but the very fabric of his existence—a humble, steadfast craft that had supported his family through the lean years and the few good ones. Yet, despite the passage of years, the clatter of the loom, and the relentless cycle of work, there remained an undercurrent of tension in his life, a thread as taut as those he worked with each day.

Will had recently reconciled with his wife, Elizabeth, but their marriage, though mended, was like a patchwork quilt—its seams visible, its fabric worn and frayed in places where the years had taken their toll. Elizabeth managed their household in Chauntry Place with a resolve forged from years of disappointment and unfulfilled dreams. Their new lodgings, a modest home nestled near Swanswell Gate, were a short walk from the river and the Swanswell Pool, where the reflection of the city shimmered on the water's surface, a mirror to the Parker family's turbulent life.

"Will, you've been at that loom since dawn," Elizabeth called out one evening, her voice a mix of concern and weariness. She stood in the doorway of their small parlour, watching her husband's steady movements as he worked. The loom's rhythmic clicking was almost hypnotic, a constant reminder of the life they had built together—one woven with care but not without its flaws.

"And where else would I be, Lizzie?" Will replied without looking up, his tone flat, as if the answer were obvious. The loom had become his refuge, a place where the complexities of life could be reduced to the simple, repetitive motion of shuttle and thread.

Elizabeth sighed, her gaze drifting to the worn rug on the floor, the chipped edges of the wooden table, and the faded curtains—all symbols of a life that had never quite met her expectations. "I only wish you'd spend as much time with the children as you do with that loom," she said softly, her voice tinged with an unspoken plea.

Will paused, the shuttle halting mid-motion. "The children," he said slowly, "they see me working, providing. Isn't that enough?"

Elizabeth shook her head, her heart aching with the knowledge that it wasn't. "They need more than that, Will. They need to know we're more than just two people living under the same roof. They need to see love, not just duty."

Their sons, Richard, now twenty-one, and Thomas, eighteen, had grown into young men—strong, capable, and quietly observant of the world around them. Their daughters, Hannah, just fifteen, and Lizzy, twelve, were on the cusp of womanhood, their eyes wide with the possibilities that life might offer, yet shadowed by the uncertainty of their parents' volatile relationship.

Hannah, in particular, had grown sensitive to the tension that ebbed and flowed in their home like the river that flowed through Swanswell Pool. She often found herself caught in the crosscurrents of her parents' emotions, struggling to make sense of the love and conflict that seemed inseparable in their household.

"Papa, are you and Mama going to argue again tonight?" Hannah asked one evening, her voice small as she stood in the doorway of the parlour, watching her father at the loom.

Will looked up, the lines on his face deepening as he took in his daughter's worried expression. "No, lass," he said gently, though the uncertainty in his heart made the words sound hollow even to him. "We're just… talking."

But Hannah knew better. She had seen too many nights where "talking" had led to raised voices, her mother's tears, and her father's silent brooding. She had seen too many reconciliations followed by fresh arguments, as if her parents were bound in a dance, they could neither master nor escape.

Despite their best efforts to shield their children from the full brunt of their marital strife, Will and Elizabeth could not hide the cracks that had formed in the foundation of their marriage. The children had become silent witnesses to the repeated breakups and reconciliations, their young lives marked by the uncertainty of whether the next day would bring peace or discord.

And yet, amidst the turbulence, there was a thread of hope—thin, perhaps, but unbroken. It was the hope that, somehow, they would find a way to weave their lives together more tightly, to mend the frayed edges of their relationship before it was too late. For now, the loom clicked on, and the family continued, imperfect but enduring, in the shadow of Swanswell Gate.

In the years following the Parker family's move to Chauntry Place, the tenuous peace in their household once again unravelled. Will and Elizabeth's marriage, already frayed and worn, tore apart again under the strain of unmet expectations and relentless disagreements. The arguments, which once ebbed and flowed like the tides, now became full-fledged storms. By the time the year 1859 dawned, Will had taken the painful step of separating from Elizabeth, leaving the family home to find lodgings elsewhere in the city. The separation, though necessary for his own sanity, left a void that Elizabeth struggled to fill.

In Will's absence, Elizabeth, ever the figure of conflicted desires, found herself drawn to the young and virile Jimmy Kimberley. Now a man of twenty, Jimmy was everything that Elizabeth's life with Will had never been—exciting, unpredictable, and charged with the kind of passion that only youth and a thirst for adventure could bring. Though Elizabeth was by now in her early forties, the years had not stripped her of her beauty or the sharpness of her wit. She had aged, yes, but like fine wine, with a complexity and allure that only deepened with time.

Jimmy, for his part, was mesmerised by Elizabeth. Her experience and maturity brought him a thrill that he had never found in the fleeting dalliances of girls his own age. There was something intoxicating about the way Elizabeth looked at him, a hunger in her eyes that matched his own. He relished the chance to play the role of the young lover, indulging in the forbidden fruit that Elizabeth offered.

It was not long before their affair became the whispered scandal of Chauntry Place. The looks exchanged between Elizabeth and Jimmy were far too lingering, their meetings far too frequent to be mere coincidence. Neighbours began to talk, their eyes narrowing with suspicion each time they saw Jimmy at Elizabeth's door. The once quiet, if uneasy, household had become a subject of gossip and judgement.

The fragile peace of their home shattered completely on one fateful Sunday evening. Driven by a gnawing sense of duty and an unresolved love for his children, Will decided to visit them at their lodgings. The separation from Elizabeth had left him adrift, and he clung to the hope that he might still be able to salvage some part of his family, if not his marriage.

As he approached the house, his heart heavy with unresolved emotions, he caught sight of Elizabeth in the front garden, conversing animatedly with Jimmy Kimberley. The sight of them together, Jimmy leaning in far too close, Elizabeth laughing in a way that Will had not seen in years sent a surge of jealousy coursing through his veins. His blood boiled, the betrayal slicing through him like a blade.

"Elizabeth!" Will's voice rang out, trembling with a mix of anger and pain. "What's this I see? You, carrying on with this lad under my very nose?" At the sight of Will, Jimmy fled.

Elizabeth, her own frustrations and desires boiling over, met Will's accusation with cold defiance. "And what if I do?" she spat back, her voice laced with venom.

Blinded by rage, Will's hand flew to her bonnet, tearing it from her head in one swift motion. "You'll bring shame upon us all, woman!" he roared, his fist striking out, the blow landing with a sickening thud that echoed in the still evening air.

Elizabeth's scream pierced the night, a sound of both shock and fury that brought the neighbours rushing to their windows and doors. The altercation, so public and so raw, ended with Will's arrest, his figure led away by the constable, his face ashen with the realisation of what he had done.

The courtroom where Will was brought to answer for his actions was a cold, unfeeling place, its walls steeped in the judgement of countless others who had come before him. Among the witnesses called was Mary Farnell, the disapproving landlady who had taken it upon herself to paint Elizabeth as a woman of loose morals, her words dripping with disdain.

"She's no better than she ought to be, your Honour," Mary declared, her voice echoing through the room. "That young Kimberley's been seen with her more times than I care to count and not in the way a decent woman would entertain a guest."

The judge, his stern face betraying no emotion, dismissed the case, attributing the entire incident to the wild jealousy of a man scorned. But the damage had been done. Will's and Elizabeth's already fragile relationship was irrevocably broken, the pieces too shattered to ever fit together again.

Yet, in the weeks that followed, as Will roamed the streets of Coventry, hollowed out by the weight of his actions and the emptiness of his new life, he found himself pulled back, once more, to the idea of reconciliation. He was exhausted—by Elizabeth's debts, her unrelenting desire for grandeur, and their endless discord cycle. But there was something else, too—a deep, abiding love for the woman he had spent his life with and for the children who were as much a part of him as the blood in his veins.

Against all odds, and despite the gossip that now followed them like a shadow, Will and Elizabeth reconciled. But it was a reconciliation born of necessity rather than genuine healing. Though no longer torn apart, the Parker household was still a battleground, its occupants weary from the constant skirmishes that marked their days.

By the summer of that year, Will's patience had worn thin. The debts had mounted, and Elizabeth's aspirations for a life they could not afford had driven him to the edge. In a final act of desperation, Will publicly declared in the Coventry Times that he would no longer be responsible for Elizabeth's financial misadventures, marking the definitive end of their tumultuous marriage. Exhausted and disillusioned, Will left the family for what he believed to be the final time, though his presence remained a haunting shadow in their lives—a ghost of the man who had tried, but ultimately failed, to keep his family together.

As the years passed, life continued to move forward, indifferent to the unfolding personal dramas. In October of 1865, Elizabeth stood on the steps of Saint Michael's Church, watching as her former lover, Jimmy Kimberley, took Catherine Marshall as his wife. The sight stirred something deep within her, a mix of regret and relief, for the passionate affair that had once consumed her had now come to an end.

Nearby, Joe Kimberley, Jimmy's father, watched Elizabeth with a disapproving eye, his discontent clear in the tight set of his jaw. For Joe, Elizabeth represented everything he had feared for his son—a woman whose influence had nearly led Jimmy astray. The ties that had once bound Jimmy and Elizabeth were now severed, but the consequences of their liaison had left a lasting mark on all involved.

As Elizabeth turned away from the church, her thoughts drifted to her daughter, Hannah, who had met a young man named William Griffiths, known as WG, that same year. Perhaps, she mused, there was hope for the next generation to find happiness where she had not. But for Elizabeth, the world had become a place of fading dreams and missed opportunities, a reflection of a life lived in the shadow of what might have been.

Martha Griffiths

Martha Griffiths was born in the tranquil village of Worthenbury, Cheshire, in 1819, where life moved with a gentle rhythm, and the ties of community ran deep. With its thatched cottages nestled among rolling green fields, the village seemed untouched by time. Yet, beneath its serene surface, life held a harshness that many villagers knew too well.

Martha's father, Richard Griffiths, was the village blacksmith whose reputation for strength, skill, and generosity made him a community pillar. The Smithy, where Martha grew up, was the heart of their world, always alive with the sound of hammer striking anvil and the warmth of the forge casting an orange glow that danced on the walls. The scent of burning coal and hot metal became as familiar to Martha as the countryside air itself.

One crisp autumn evening, when the leaves crunched underfoot like brittle parchment, and the air carried a bite of the coming winter, young Martha, then just ten years old, sat on a low stool near the forge. She watched with wide, curious eyes as her father worked, the sparks flying in a golden shower each time his hammer met the iron. The glow of the fire cast a magical hue, turning the humble Smithy into a place of wonder in Martha's young mind.

Richard Griffiths paused his work for a moment, wiping the sweat from his brow with a soot-stained handkerchief. His face, worn and lined from years of hard labour, softened as he glanced at his daughter, her small frame bathed in the warm light of the fire.

"Father," Martha began, her voice a mix of innocence and admiration, "will I ever be as strong as you?"

Richard chuckled, a deep, comforting sound filling the small space of the forge. He knelt beside her, placing a heavy hand on her shoulder. "Strength, my dear Martha, isn't just in the arms," he said, his voice gentle yet firm. It's in here." He tapped his chest over his heart. "One day, you'll be stronger than me, in ways neither of us can yet see."

Martha held onto those words as the years passed, drawing strength from them as life around her grew more demanding.

At just ten years old, Martha faced the devastating loss of her mother, Elizabeth Burton, an event that would cast a long shadow over her childhood. Elizabeth had been the heart of the household; her gentle presence and nurturing love provided a sense of security and warmth that wrapped around the family like a protective blanket. She was the one who soothed the children's fears, tended to their needs, and filled their home with laughter and comfort, even amidst the hardships of daily life.

But when Elizabeth fell ill, the atmosphere in the house began to change. What started as a mild sickness soon turned into something more serious, and despite their best efforts to care for her, Elizabeth's condition deteriorated rapidly. Martha, though still a child, sensed the gravity of the situation. She watched with growing fear as her mother, once so strong and full of life, became increasingly frail, her energy slipping away day by day.

The day Elizabeth passed was a day Martha would never forget. The house, usually bustling with the sounds of a busy family, fell eerily silent. The stillness was broken only by the muffled cries of her siblings and the heavy footsteps of her father as he paced the floor, his grief too immense to express in words. Martha sat by her mother's bedside, clutching Elizabeth's hand, willing her to wake up, smile at her one more time, and say that everything would be alright. But that moment never came.

When Elizabeth took her last breath, it felt as though the very life had been drained from the room. The warmth that had once permeated their home was replaced by a coldness that even the roaring fire in the forge could not dispel. Once anchored by her mother's steady presence, Martha's world was suddenly adrift. The loss of Elizabeth was not just the loss of a mother but the loss of the family's emotional centre.

In the days that followed, the house seemed emptier and quieter, as if the joy had been permanently extinguished. The siblings clung to each other, trying to fill the void that Elizabeth had left behind, but it was a gap that could never truly be closed. For Martha, the loss was especially profound. At ten years old, she was old enough to understand the permanence of death but too young to fully grasp how to navigate the world without her mother's guidance.

Though he did his best to maintain a sense of normalcy, her father was clearly struggling with his own grief. He continued to work in the forge, the rhythmic pounding of metal on metal a constant in their lives, but there was a sadness in his eyes that Martha had never seen before. The forge, once a place of warmth and creation, now seemed a place of escape where he could momentarily forget the pain of his loss.

Martha found herself taking on responsibilities beyond her years, trying to fill the void left by her mother. She helped care for her family, prepared meals, and attempted to keep the household running, but the burden was heavy for someone so young. The grief, still raw and fresh, lingered like a cloud over their lives, and though the passage of time would eventually soften the edges of their pain, the loss of Elizabeth would leave an indelible mark on Martha's heart, shaping the woman she would one day become.

By the age of sixteen, Martha had taken on many of the household responsibilities, her hands now accustomed to the daily grind of chores and the relentless rhythm of village life. She worked alongside her father and brothers, proving her worth through her dedication and resilience.

One chilly morning, as she hung freshly washed clothes on the line, the crisp air biting at her cheeks, Martha's thoughts wandered beyond the boundaries of their village. The longing in her heart for something more, something beyond the life she knew, began to surface. She turned to her older brother, George, who was helping her with the washing.

"George," she began, her voice filled with a quiet yearning, "do you ever wonder what lies beyond Worthenbury? Beyond these fields and cottages?"

George paused, his hands busy pinning a sheet to the line, and frowned slightly. Ever the protective elder, his brow furrowed in thought. "The world is vast, Martha," he replied, his tone cautious. "But it's not always kind. You might find excitement out there, but you'll also find dangers you can't even imagine. Here, we have each other, and that's more important than anything beyond our village."

Martha nodded, though her eyes still held that faraway look. "But don't you ever wonder, George? What would it be like to see the places we've only heard about? To live a life different from this?"

George sighed, his expression softening as he looked at his sister. "Maybe I do, sometimes," he admitted, his voice lowering to a conspiratorial whisper. "But it's dangerous to want more than what you have. Ambition can lead you astray, Martha. Remember that."

Despite George's warnings, Martha couldn't shake the feeling that there was something more waiting for her beyond the familiar confines of Worthenbury. Yet, despite the hardships, a sense of hope and determination ran through the Griffiths household—a belief that, as long as they were together, they could weather any storm.

The bond between Martha and George grew even stronger in the wake of their mother's death. They leaned on each other, drawing comfort and strength from their shared memories and their mutual resolve to honour their parents' legacy.

"Martha," George said one evening as they sat by the dying embers of the fire, the weight of the day heavy on their shoulders, "we'll get through this, you and I. Father would want us to carry on, to keep the forge burning in our hearts, even if it's not in the Smithy."

Martha nodded, her eyes glistening with unshed tears. "We will, George. For Mother. For all of us."

And so, life in Worthenbury went on. The seasons changed, and with them, the fortunes of the Griffiths family. But through it all, the bond between Martha and George remained unbroken, a testament to the strength their parents had instilled in them.

One bright summer day when Martha was about eighteen, she accompanied her older brother, George, on some routine errands to the neighbouring village of Sarn. They had undertaken the journey countless times, but this outing held a unique charm as it allowed them a rare moment of respite from the relentless demands of their lives at the Smithy. Their bond, forged through hardship and shared experiences, made these excursions a cherished escape from their daily routines.

As they walked along the winding paths to Sarn, George, always the more cautious of the two, warned Martha about taking a shortcut through Threapwood on her early return home, a place known for its dubious reputation. The dense woods of Threapwood had a history of lawlessness and danger, but Martha, eager to hasten their return and dismissive of George's concerns.

"George," she said, her voice light and carefree, "I'll be back before you know it. We've made this journey countless times; what could go wrong?"

George's brow furrowed with worry, but he reluctantly agreed. "Alright, Martha, keep your wits about you. Threapwood isn't the safest of places."

George's eyes lingered on Martha as they parted ways, a premonition of dread tugging at his heart. Martha walked into the woods, her footsteps quick and determined, though a shadow of unease followed her.

But the danger that lurked in Threapwood was far worse than anyone could have anticipated. As she navigated the dense underbrush, a figure emerged from the darkness, and Martha's world was turned upside down. The brutal assault that followed left her shattered, both physically and emotionally. The attack was swift and violent, leaving her with deep, unhealable wounds that went far beyond the physical.

George, realising too late the folly of allowing Martha to take the shortcut alone, found her after the attack. The sight of his sister, battered and broken, filled him with a profound sense of guilt and helplessness. With trembling hands, he carried her back home, his heart heavy with remorse.

Back at the Smithy that evening, the sight of Martha's broken form left the Griffiths family reeling. Richard Griffiths, the family's anchor, knelt beside his daughter, his eyes filled with anguish as he tried to comfort her.

"Martha, my brave girl," he said, his voice breaking, "you are not defined by what has happened to you. Your strength and your heart remain unbroken. We are here for you, always."

Martha looked at her father, her eyes brimming with tears. "But Father, how do I face the world again? How do I find strength when everything inside me feels so hollow?"

Richard took her hands in his, his rough palms warm and steady against her trembling skin. "One day at a time, my dear. And remember, you have us, your family. We stand by you, always."

The trauma of the assault left Martha Griffiths deeply scarred, a silent battle she fought daily with a grim resolve. The weight of her ordeal pressed heavily upon her, each day a struggle against the shadows of her past. When Martha discovered she was pregnant, her despair grew darker, the cruel twist of fate adding yet another layer to her suffering.

In 1837, she gave birth to a daughter, Jane, born of the violence inflicted upon her in Threapwood. The identity of the father remained a veiled secret, a painful truth Martha could neither speak of nor escape. The stigma of her situation was a heavy shroud that obscured her future, and she bore the burden of her silent anguish with a stoic endurance that belied her inner turmoil.

The following winter, Richard Griffiths fell ill when the frost lay thick on the ground, and the hearths burned brightly to keep the cold at bay. The robust and unyielding man who had once seemed invincible now lay bedridden, his once-vibrant spirit dimmed by sickness. Martha and George nursed him with all the care and love they could muster, but the illness was relentless.

"Father," Martha whispered one night as she sat by his bedside, her voice choked with tears she refused to shed, "you're the strongest man I know. You'll get through this, won't you?"

Richard, his voice weak but his spirit still resolute, managed a faint smile. "Remember what I told you, Martha," he said, his breath coming in laboured gasps. "Strength isn't just in the arms... it's in the heart. You have that strength, my girl. Never forget it."

Richard passed away before the winter thawed, leaving a void in the Griffiths household that could never be filled. The forge, once the beating heart of their home, fell silent, the anvil cold and unused. Martha, though heartbroken, took her father's words to heart. She steeled herself, knowing she had to be strong for herself and her family.

George stepped up as the man of the house, and his bond with Martha only grew stronger after their father's death. They leaned on each other, drawing comfort and strength from their shared memories and mutual resolve to honour Richard's legacy. However, the community's judgment over her having a child out of wedlock compounded her grief, and she felt compelled to remove herself from the scrutiny that had begun to sour her life. Now, the head of the family, George, was left to manage the Smithy and the household, relieved of the additional burden of public condemnation.

Martha sought refuge and a fresh start in Meriden, Warwickshire. She had known William Griffiths from her days in Worthenbury—though he was not related to her—William had always held a torch for her. He had moved to Meriden to work on the railways, and Martha, guided by his suggestion and recommendation, decided to relocate there.

William welcomed Martha with warmth and kindness, offering her a glimmer of hope amidst her turmoil. As they grew closer, their bond strengthened, though Martha remained wary, her past casting a long shadow over her heart. William's affections were sincere, and his support gave Martha a much-needed respite from her sorrow.

One evening, as they walked together by the village green in Meriden, William turned to Martha, his gaze filled with sincere affection. "Martha, you have endured so much, and yet you carry yourself with such resilience. Let us build a future together—a future for us, for Jane, and our children."

Martha's heart, though cautious, responded to his words. She looked at him with a mixture of hope and wariness. "William, if there is one thing I have learned, hope can be found even in the darkest times. Together, we can face whatever comes."

Martha and William's relationship was one built on mutual respect but carried the weight of Martha's past traumas. Martha kept William at a cautious distance, her heart guarded by the scars of an assault that had shaken her ability to trust fully. Her hesitancy turned their marriage into more of a companionship than a deeply passionate union. Though William longed for a more intimate and loving connection, he never pressured her for more than she was willing to give. His actions were always respectful, honoring her boundaries, and treating her with the utmost care and gentleness.

William, though gentlemanly in every sense, could not hide the yearning for the closeness that seemed just out of reach. He was patient, understanding that Martha's need for emotional distance stemmed from her past, but the ache for a deeper bond still lingered in his heart. Despite the unspoken gap between them, their relationship was one of quiet support—steady, if not deeply romantic. In the small moments of everyday life, they found comfort in each other's presence, even if the connection was not the passionate love that William might have dreamed of.

In 1843, Martha gave birth to a son, William Griffiths Jr. (WG). Though she did not name WG's father on the birth certificate, Martha focused on her children with unwavering dedication, determined to provide them with the love and stability she had found so lacking in her life.

Through the trials and tribulations, Martha remained steadfast in her resolve to give her children a better life. The scars of her past were a part of her, but they did not define her. With her family's support and William's companionship, Martha faced each day with quiet strength, carving out a place of solace and hope amidst the turbulence of her past.

In 1849, as Martha and William faced increasing hardship and struggled to make ends meet, they were forced to confront a painful reality—they could no longer adequately provide for Jane. At twelve years old, Jane needed more stability than their poverty-stricken home could offer. With heavy hearts, Martha approached her brother George, asking if he could take Jane in.

George, driven by his own sense of guilt over Martha's past suffering, didn't hesitate. He felt responsible for easing his sister's burden and saw caring for Jane not only as an obligation but also as a way of making amends for what he believed were his own failings in the past. For George, welcoming Jane into his home in Worthenbury was not just about offering her a better life, but also a way to atone for the suffering he believed Martha had endured because of him.

This decision marked the beginning of a new chapter for Jane, one that would provide her with the stability and care her parents could no longer offer. While it was a painful separation, both Martha and William found some comfort in knowing that Jane would be in safe hands, even if it meant letting her go.

One sunny afternoon, as George and Jane sat in the modest kitchen of the Smithy, George placed a reassuring hand on her shoulder. The forge's warm glow bathed them in a soft light, and the rhythmic clanging of the anvil echoed his earnest words.

"Jane," George began, his voice tinged with both regret and resolve, "I failed your mother once, and the weight of that failure has never left me. But I swear to you, I will not fail you. This is your home now; you will always have a place here as long as I draw breath."

Jane, her face illuminated by the flickering light of the hearth, looked up at her uncle with eyes that held a reflection of her mother's indomitable spirit. Her voice, though soft, carried the strength of her lineage.

"Thank you, Uncle George," she said, a hint of a smile touching her lips. "Mother always says that family is our greatest strength, and I believe she was right. It means so much to me to have a place where I am wanted."

George's heart swelled with a mix of sorrow and relief. He was determined to provide Jane with the stability and care that had been so cruelly denied to Martha. As they continued their conversation, George shared stories of their ancestors, the forge, and the village's past—stories that bound Jane to her heritage and gave her a sense of belonging.

As days turned into months, Jane began to settle into her new life. The Smithy, once silent and melancholic, became a place of new beginnings. Though still haunted by the past, George found solace in his niece's laughter and presence. The rhythms of the forge, the familiar clang of metal, and the warmth of the hearth now carried a new promise: the promise of healing, redemption, and a future where the family bonds could soften the past's shadows.

By 1851, Martha, William, and WG were living in the Poor House on Maxstoke Lane in Meriden. Despite Martha's unwavering determination and tireless efforts to provide for WG, their circumstances were bleak. Work nearby was becoming scarce, and the local economy offered little in the way of improvement. The prospect of a better future seemed increasingly distant in their current environment.

Martha considered a move to Liverpool—fuelled by necessity and hope. The city was rapidly becoming a hub of commerce and industry, with its bustling docks and vibrant economy presenting opportunities that Meriden could not offer. Martha had learned of the possibilities that awaited in Liverpool through her mother's relatives, the Burtons, who had moved there and established themselves in the city. Their support was pivotal in her decision-making process, offering a potential place to stay and a connection to a network that could help her and WG get a fresh start.

In addition to the lure of work on the docks and railways, which promised better wages and more stable employment, Martha was drawn to Liverpool by the city's thriving textile industry. As a skilled seamstress, she saw a chance to make a more substantial income and provide a better life for WG and with William at her side. The Burtons had spoken of the city's bustling markets and the demand for skilled workers, which gave Martha hope that her skills would be in high demand.

Before the move, Martha wrote to her daughter in Worthenbury. In her heartfelt letter, Martha detailed the reasons behind their decision:

"Dear Jane," Martha began, her handwriting steady but tinged with emotion, "I hope this letter finds you in good spirits. Life in Meriden has become increasingly challenging, and I've realised that our prospects here are limited. I've decided to move to Liverpool, a city full of opportunity and promise. The docks are bustling with activity and a growing demand for skilled workers. With the support of our Burton relatives, who have generously offered us a place to stay, I believe this move will provide us with the fresh start we so desperately need."

She continued, explaining the practical aspects of the move and her hopes for the future. "Liverpool is thriving, and the opportunities it offers are too great to ignore. I have heard from the Burtons about the work available on the docks and in the textile industry, which aligns perfectly with my skills as a seamstress. This is a chance for us to build a new life and secure a better future."

Martha's letter concluded with a heartfelt invitation. "I know this news may come as a surprise, but I am confident this change will benefit us all. I eagerly await the day when we can be reunited. Please consider joining us in Liverpool when you are able. Your presence will bring immense joy to my heart, and together, we can forge a new beginning."

Martha, WG, and William Griffiths prepared for their journey to Liverpool, the decision to move driven by the promise of new opportunities and the support of the Burton family. The bustling port city symbolised a beacon of hope, offering the potential for a better life and a fresh start. Liverpool's vibrant economy and the Burtons' assistance encouraged Martha to take this bold step, seeking a brighter future for herself and her children.

As she packed her belongings, Jane felt a tangled web of hope and sorrow. The small room she had called home with her Uncle George felt suddenly foreign, its familiar comforts overshadowed by the looming uncertainty of her future. The thought of leaving behind the man who had become her father was almost too much to bear, yet the pull to reunite with her mother, William, and young WG in Liverpool was equally strong.

George approached her with a solemn expression, his usually steady hands trembling ever so slightly as he reached out to touch her shoulder. His heart was heavy with the weight of their impending separation, a sadness he couldn't fully express.

"Jane," George said softly, his voice thick with emotion as he wrapped his arms around her in a heartfelt embrace, "you carry with you the love and strength of this family. Remember, no matter where you go, that love will guide you."

Jane clung to him, burying her face in his chest, her tears soaking into the rough fabric of his shirt. The scent of the forge, the hard work and dedication that had defined their life together, was a comfort she feared she would never find again.

"I will, Uncle George," she whispered, her voice breaking with the weight of her emotions. "I promise I'll make you proud and keep the family's spirit alive."

George's voice trembled slightly as he replied, "You've always been a beacon of strength, Jane. Your mother will be fortunate to have you by her side." He pulled back slightly, his eyes searching hers as if trying to memorise every detail of her face. "Remember, you'll always have a home here, with me, in Worthenbury."

Jane nodded, but the decision was tearing her apart. The longing to be with her mother, to support her in Liverpool, was undeniable. Yet, the thought of leaving George behind, of walking away from the only home she had indeed known, filled her with dread.

The morning of her departure arrived far too quickly. Jane stood in the doorway, her small bag packed with all she owned, her heart heavy with the knowledge that she was leaving behind a part of herself. George stood by the gate, trying to hide the tears that threatened to spill from his eyes.

"Take care of yourself, Jane," he said, his voice barely above a whisper. "And remember, this isn't goodbye. You're just following your heart."

With a final, emotional farewell, Jane left for Liverpool, carrying the legacy of her family's love and support. The journey was long, but her mind was a whirlwind of thoughts and memories. She couldn't shake the feeling of being torn between two worlds—one rooted in the past and the other in the uncertain future.

When she finally arrived in Liverpool, the city's vibrant energy and endless possibilities starkly contrasted with the quiet life she had left behind. The bustling streets and towering ships in the docks were overwhelming, yet they also promised something new that could be better than she had known.

One evening, as they gathered in their modest home, the familiar hum of the bustling city outside reminded them of their new surroundings. Jane turned to her mother, her voice filled with admiration and uncertainty.

"Mother," Jane began hesitantly, her gaze steady and heartfelt, "you've given us so much. How do you find the strength to keep going despite everything?"

Martha, her hands busy with the needlework of her seamstress trade, looked up with a warm, enduring smile that belied her hardships. "Jane, my strength comes from you and WG. You both are my heart and soul. As long as I have you both by my side, I have the strength to face anything life throws our way."

Jane's eyes shone with a mixture of love and gratitude and a lingering sadness for the life she had left behind. "We'll face it together, Mother," she said softly. "No matter what comes our way, we have each other."

Martha reached over, gently squeezing Jane's hand. "And that's all we need, my dear."

Though starting anew, the Griffiths family found solace and hope amidst Liverpool's bustling streets and dynamic docks. Martha's resilience and strong bond with her children anchored their lives. Yet, even in this new life, Jane's heart was still divided, her thoughts often drifting back to Worthenbury and the uncle she had left behind.

As they settled into their new life, Jane wrote frequent letters to George, sharing stories of their life in Liverpool and their challenges. Each letter was a thread, a way to stay connected to the life she had known, even as she built a new one with her mother and WG.

In the city's heart, amidst the clamour and chaos, Jane began to find her place, but she never forgot the quiet strength and love of the home she had left behind. While Martha discovered a sense of belonging and purpose, her legacy was not just one of resilience and hope but also of the deep, unbreakable bonds that tied their family together, no matter the distance.

William Griffiths Jr. (WG)

Born in 1843 in the humble village of Meriden near Coventry, young William Griffiths Jr. entered a world fraught with hardship. The modesty of his birthplace, a small village nestled amid the rolling English countryside, belied the challenges that awaited him. From the very beginning, his life was a struggle against the odds.

To prevent confusion from the outset, William Jr. was affectionately known as WG—a distinction that became necessary due to the presence of his father, also named William. The initials "WG" not only served to avoid the inevitable mix-ups in conversation but also set young William apart, giving him an identity that, while tied to his father, was uniquely his own. This simple moniker would become a badge of resilience, a symbol of the quiet determination that would define his life.

WG's early years in Meriden were marked by poverty. The family's circumstances were meagre, with little more than the bare necessities to sustain them. WG's mother, Martha, worked tirelessly to keep the family afloat, her hands always busy with needlework or any odd job that could bring in a few extra shillings. Life was a daily grind, with the spectre of hunger never far from their door.

The village, though picturesque, could be harsh to those who were different or vulnerable. With his shy demeanour and patched clothing, WG quickly became the target of the village bullies. He was often taunted for his family's poverty, worn boots, and ragged clothes hanging loosely on his small frame. The other children, with their cruel, unthinking jibes, made sure that WG never forgot his place on the lowest rung of society.

Despite the bullying, WG found solace in his elder half-sister, Jane (whom he lovingly called Janie). Janie was a beacon of strength in his young life, always ready with a kind word or a protective arm. She had a natural warmth about her, a quiet assurance that life, however harsh, could be borne with dignity. When WG would come home after a particularly rough day, his spirit battered and bruised, it was Janie who would sit with him by the hearth, her presence alone a comfort in the darkness.

"Don't let them get to you, WG," Janie would say, her voice steady and filled with conviction. "You're stronger than they'll ever know. And one day, you'll rise above all of this. You'll see."

Her words, though simple, planted a seed of resilience in WG's heart. He clung to them on the worst days when the weight of the world seemed too heavy for a child to bear.

The year 1849 brought a profound loss for young WG when his beloved half-sister, Janie, left for Worthenbury. At just six years old, WG was left to grapple with the sudden absence of his elder sister who had offered him comfort and protection amidst their poverty-stricken life. Janie's departure was a blow to his already fragile world, leaving him feeling more isolated than ever. Without her calming presence and reassuring words, WG faced the daily challenges of his harsh surroundings with a heavier heart. Her absence marked the beginning of a brief lonely chapter in his young life, as the only person who understood and protected him was no longer by his side.

By 1851, the Griffiths family could no longer endure the relentless hardships of Meriden. The village that had once seemed so peaceful had become a place of unyielding struggle. The lure of better prospects led them to Liverpool, a bustling city that promised opportunity and a fresh start. The decision to move was not made lightly, but the crushing poverty and the constant bullying left them with little choice.

The move to Liverpool marked a turning point in WG's life. The city, with its crowded streets and towering ships, was a world away from the quiet fields of Meriden. There was an energy in the air, a sense that anything was possible if one was willing to work for it. For WG, it was both daunting and exhilarating.

In Liverpool, WG's mother, Martha, found work as a seamstress. Her nimble fingers stitched together a future for her children, one thread at a time. Though the work was hard, there was a new hope in her heart, a belief that they could finally escape the shadow of poverty that had loomed over them for so long.

Meanwhile, Janie—reunited with the family—had found her place in service with the help of the Burton family. Her position, though modest, provided her with a sense of purpose and a measure of independence. She continued to be a source of unwavering support for WG, always encouraging him to find his own path in the bustling city.

"Liverpool is a place of opportunity, WG," Janie would tell him as they walked through the bustling streets, the noise of the docks a constant backdrop to their conversations. "It's rough and tough, but if you keep your wits about you and work hard, you can make something of yourself here."

WG listened to her words, the same quiet determination that had seen him through the trials of Meriden growing stronger within him. He knew that life in Liverpool would not be easy, but for the first time, he felt that perhaps he could carve out a place for himself in the world—a place where he was not defined by his poverty or his past but by the strength of his character and the choices he made.

The years that followed were not without their challenges, but with Janie's guidance and his mother's unwavering love, WG began to forge his own path in the sprawling city. The hardships of his early years had left their mark, but they had also given him a resilience that would serve him well in the years to come. And though he was just a boy when he arrived in Liverpool, by the time he began to find his footing, he had already shown a glimpse of the man he would one day become—a man defined not by his circumstances but by his enduring spirit and the strength of his family's love.

Liverpool, a throbbing hub of industry and commerce, offered young William a world of new opportunities. The city's ceaseless energy, with its bustling docks, clanging factories, and endless streams of people from every walk of life, was a far cry from the quiet fields of Meriden, where he had spent his earliest years. Here, in the heart of this industrial giant, William's horizons began to expand, his curiosity sparked by the myriad possibilities that the city presented.

At fifteen, WG found himself drawn to the intricate world of watchmaking. With its delicate precision and meticulous craftsmanship, the trade captured his imagination like nothing else had before. He would often linger outside the small watchmaker's shops in the city, peering through the windows at the skilled artisans as they worked, their nimble fingers assembling the tiny gears and springs that made up the heart of a timepiece. There was something almost magical about how they could take such small, seemingly insignificant parts and bring them together to create a machine that could measure time.

One day, while wandering the streets after work, WG came across a small workshop tucked away in a narrow alley. The sign above the door read "Byron's Timepieces." Intrigued, he stepped inside and was immediately enveloped by the rich scent of oil and metal. Behind the counter stood Thomas Byron. An older man with sharp eyes and a steady hand was bent over a bench, carefully assembling a watch. The man looked up and smiled as WG entered, the wrinkles around his eyes crinkling, suggesting he had spent a lifetime perfecting his craft.

"What can I do for you, lad?" the man asked, his voice gruff but not unkind.

WG hesitated, his heart pounding in his chest. "I—I'm interested in watchmaking," he stammered. "I've been watching the craftsmen at work, and I think I'd like to learn."

The man studied him for a long moment before nodding slowly. "It's a demanding trade, requires patience and a steady hand. But it can be a rewarding life if you've got the passion for it."

This simple conversation planted the seed of a dream in WG's heart—a dream that he carried with him as he continued to navigate the challenges of his young life in Liverpool. But the path to becoming a watchmaker was not straightforward. WG knew he would need guidance, training, and perhaps most importantly, the support of others who shared his ambition.

It was whilst working at Byron's that WG became close friends with Tom Green and Tom's elder brother, Dickie. The Green brothers, like WG, were full of hope and dreams for a future brighter than the one they had known. Thomas had taught them the basics of watchmaking, and the three young men spent countless hours discussing their plans, huddled together in the dimly lit corners of the Byron workshop after the day's work was done.

One day, WG, leaning over the workbench, examining a finely wrought timepiece, said, "Tom, have you ever seen such precision? The way each gear fits into the next, every movement perfectly timed... it's as if the watch breathes life itself." Tom, nodding thoughtfully, his fingers tracing the edge of a brass cog, "Aye, Will, there's a beauty in the craft, no doubt. But I often wonder—what good is a skill so fine if we're shackled by the Truck Act? We toil, and yet, we're paid in tokens like children. It's a fair mockery." Dickie, seated by the window, his gaze distant as he contemplates their future, "Liverpool's been kind enough, I suppose, but the air here—it's thick with soot and desperation. I've heard they tell of Coventry, though—a city where fortunes are spun as quickly as thread. They say the men there work with freedom, not these cursed tokens. Imagine it, lads, earning your keep in honest coin, not the pittance these masters dole out". WG, his eyes bright with ambition, "Coventry, you say? It's a tantalising thought, Dickie. A place where a man's skill is worth its weight in gold, not in some paltry chit. Perhaps there lies the key to our futures—a place where we could shape our own destinies, free from the binds of this industry." Tom, a smile playing at his lips, "Aye, Will, Coventry may well be the answer. If we take what we've learned here, apply it where men are free to make their fortunes... Why, we could be masters of our own trade, not slaves to the whims of another."

Dickie, standing, his voice resolute, "Then it's settled. Liverpool's taught us well, but it's Coventry where our future lies. Let us forge ahead, lads, with hope in our hearts and the skill of our hands as our guide. The road may be long, but with each tick of the clock, we draw nearer to our fortunes."

WG, raising his hand as if to seal their pact, "To Coventry, then, and to the bright future it promises. May we find the opportunities that elude us here in that fair city, and may our names be spoken of in the same breath as the greatest craftsmen."

Tom and Dickie, in unison, their voices full of determination and laughter, "To Coventry!"

The three boys exchanged a knowing look, their hearts filled with the promise of a brighter tomorrow as the sun set over the smoky rooftops of Liverpool, casting long shadows on their chosen path.

On a cold evening, the kind that seeped into your bones and made you doubt the existence of warmth. WG found himself near the corner of Hillock Street, not with any particular purpose, just lingering with Tom and Dickie as they often did. The day seemed unremarkable until he noticed a makeshift ring being set up in the muddy square, already drawing a crowd eager for a bit of excitement to chase away the chill.

Ever the instigator, Tom nudged WG with a grin promising mischief. "Look there, WG! Some traveller boys are bragging about being unbeaten. Says he can take on anyone brave enough to step into that ring. How about you show him what those fists of yours can do?"

WG glanced at the lad—a stout, burly figure, already stripped to the waist, shadowboxing as if he owned the air around him. For a moment, a flicker of doubt crossed WG's mind. He had never fought beyond a bit of sparring in the back alleys, never put himself on display like this. But the thrill of the challenge quickly began to drown out that doubt.

"I don't know, Tom," WG muttered, more to himself than to anyone else. "I've only fought for fun, but if he's so sure of himself…"

Dickie, always the one to see an opportunity, leaned in with a sly smile. "There's money in this, WG. Not just from the fight. You win, and the bets will come pouring in. Everyone around here loves a good wager, especially on a sure thing."

Determination settled in WG's chest, solid as stone. "Alright, lads. Let's see if this Irish boy can handle a real fight."

As the bout began, the crowd buzzed with anticipation, their breath hanging in the air like mist. The traveller came out swinging, all brute force and bluster, his fists flying with the reckless energy of a young bull. WG kept light on his feet, dodging the wild punches, his mind sharp and focused. Tom and Dickie stood just outside the ring, their hearts pounding in rhythm with the fight.

For the first few minutes, it was a test of endurance. WG danced around his opponent, waiting for the right moment to strike. The traveller grew frustrated, his blows becoming sloppier with each missed attempt. That was when WG made his move—quick, precise jabs that landed square on the traveller's jaw and ribs. The crowd gasped, surprised by the skill shown by this unassuming lad from Sparling Street.

"Get in there, WG!" Tom shouted, his voice cutting through the noise. "Show him what you're made of!"

The traveller boy staggered, his bravado slipping as he struggled to keep up with WG's speed and accuracy. WG saw the moment when the boy's confidence broke, and he didn't hesitate. A final, powerful uppercut sent the boy crashing to the ground. The fight was over, and the crowd erupted in a mix of shock and applause.

WG stood in the middle of that makeshift ring, breath coming heavy but heart steady. He had done it. Tom and Dickie rushed over, slapping him on the back, pride written all over their faces.

"You did it, WG!" Dickie exclaimed, his eyes gleaming with excitement. "We've got ourselves a champion! The bets are coming in thick and fast—we'll be living like kings tonight!"

WG nodded, still catching his breath but already feeling the weight of what this victory could mean. This fight had been more than just a test of strength; it had offered a glimpse of a future where he could rise above the hardships of their world, one punch at a time.

Once calloused from hours spent tinkering with pocket watches, his fists had found a new purpose that night. And standing in that ring, WG knew this was just the beginning.

The arrival of Frances in the spring of 1858 breathed new life into the Griffiths household. Her birth brought a long-awaited sense of wholeness, finally completing a family that had once been marked by difficult beginnings. William and Martha, having faced their share of hardships, found renewed joy in their youngest daughter, who seemed to symbolise a fresh chapter for them. Their home on Sparling Street, already filled with the lively energy of her elder siblings, felt warmer and more alive with the promise of this new addition.

WG had just turned fifteen and eagerly embraced the role of protector. His bond with his little sister was instant, as if he understood that her presence was the final piece needed to mend old wounds. Meanwhile, Janie, now a young woman, adored Frances from the moment she laid eyes on her. With a wisdom that came from having witnessed the family's struggles, she lavished her younger sister with the kind of love that only deepens over time.

For the entire family, Frances became a symbol of unity and hope, the tender force that seemed to pull them all closer. WG and Janie, both fiercely devoted in their own ways, wrapped her in a cocoon of love and protection. Though still an infant, Frances was already the heart of the household, the precious piece that had long been missing. Her presence was not just a new beginning, but the fulfillment of a family bond that had been waiting to fully bloom.

In 1861, at eighteen, WG decided to leave for Coventry, seeking a brighter future through his trade. His departure marked a significant change for the family, leaving a bittersweet feeling in their home on Sparling Street. Though WG was eager to carve his own path and pursue new opportunities, he couldn't shake the thought of the cocoon of family warmth Frances had brought into their lives. Over the past three years, his youngest sister had become the heart of their household, and he knew he would miss the special bond that had developed. However, WG promised himself that he would return often, unwilling to fully sever the ties that tightly bound him to his beloved family.

WG's move to Coventry left behind not just Frances, but also Tom and Dickie. Tom had recently found love with Jane Byron, the daughter of Thomas Byron, and was ready to begin a new chapter of his own. Their relationship brought the family fresh hope, even as they faced the changes brought by WG's departure. Meanwhile, Dickie, ever practical and forward-thinking, was contemplating a significant shift in his own career. He considered applying his mechanical skills to the small arms industry in Birmingham, a burgeoning field that promised new prospects.

Witnessing their children's growth and pursuit of their futures was a collective experience for William and Martha. WG's departure left a noticeable gap, but they were united in understanding his ambitions. As the family adapted to these changes, the home on Sparling Street remained a symbol of the enduring love that Frances's arrival had sparked, a love that would bind them together through life's transitions.

Settling in at 10 Barras Lane, Coventry, under the roof of William Fullwell, a silk weaver, WG's days were consumed with the meticulous art of watch finishing, honing his skills amidst the clatter of machinery and the scent of raw silk that permeated the air. Through Fullwell, WG first encountered Hannah Parker, a spirited girl weaver from a respected silk-weaving family residing in the newly developed Chauntry Place.

Hannah's presence at the Golden Cross Inn, where she worked in the evening, caught WG's eye from the outset. Fresh from Liverpool, he quickly earned a reputation as a tough and determined young man. His evenings often found him at the inn, engaged in flirtatious banter with Hannah, whose charm and wit captivated him deeply. One fateful night, their playful exchanges split out into the quiet streets of Pepper Lane, and their passion ignited under the watchful spires of Holy Trinity Church.

William, leaning casually against the bar, his eyes fixed on Hannah as she pours ale for a patron, "Miss Parker, it seems you have a knack for making a man forget his woes. I dare say the day's labours feel lighter in your presence." With a teasing smile, not missing a beat as she slides the mug across the counter, "Aye, sir, it's said that laughter and good company are the finest cures for a weary soul. And from what I hear, you've no shortage of either."

WG, chuckling, leans in closer, lowering his voice to a conspiratorial whisper, "Perhaps, but I find myself in need of something more... substantial. A charm like yours, Hannah, could lift a man from the depths of despair." Blushing slightly, though her voice remained playful, "Is that so? Or is it that the ale is working its magic and not the barmaid?"

WG, grinning, "Ah, you wound me, Miss Parker. My senses are as sharp as any. No, it's not the ale, but the lady behind it that draws me here night after night."

Hannah, meeting his gaze with a mischievous glint in her eye, "Words are easy, WG. Show me a man's deeds, and I'll tell you his heart."

WG, his voice softening, full of sincerity, "Then let me prove it, Hannah. Let me walk you home tonight, and perhaps you'll see the truth of my words."

Hannah paused for a moment, weighing his offer, then nodded with a playful arch of her brow. "Very well, but mind you, I've no need of a chaperone. The streets of Coventry hold no fear for me."

They left the warm glow of the inn behind, stepping into the cool night air. The cobbled streets of Pepper Lane were quiet, save for the distant murmur of voices and the occasional clatter of a horse's hooves. As they walk side by side, their playful banter gave way to a comfortable silence, the only sound of the soft rustle of their footsteps.

WG, glancing up at the towering spires of Holy Trinity Church as they approach. "This city is full of secrets, don't you think? Stories in every stone, shadows that tell of lives lived and lost."

Hannah, following his gaze, her voice thoughtful. "Aye, secrets indeed. Some best left buried, others waiting to be discovered... much like the heart, wouldn't you say?"

WG, catching the note of seriousness in her tone, steps closer, his hand brushing hers. "And what secrets does your heart hold, Hannah? What would it reveal if only given the chance?"

Turning to face him, her expression softened, though there was a spark of challenge in her eyes. "Perhaps... that it's been waiting for something—or someone—to stir it from its slumber."

Their gazes lock, and at that moment, the world around them seems to fade into nothingness. Without another word, they move together, the distance between them closing until their lips meet in a fierce, passionate kiss. The ancient stones of the churchyard bear silent witness as their desire overtakes them, the night air thick with the heady scent of blooming roses and the thrill of something forbidden.

Hannah, pulling back slightly, her breath coming in quick gasps, whispers against his lips. "This... this isn't the first time these grounds have seen such things. My own mother... she spoke of a night like this long ago."

His voice was low, full of yearning and a newfound tenderness. "Then let us not waste a moment more, Hannah. Let this night be ours, a secret shared with the shadows and the stars."

With a final, searing kiss, they give in to the pull of their passion, their bodies intertwining under the watchful spires of the church as if bound by the very history that surrounds them.

The consequences of that night reverberated deeply. In 1862, Elizabeth Parker Griffiths entered the world, a testament to their fleeting moment of passion. Determined to write the course, WG and Hannah tied the knot in Holy Trinity on May 18, 1864. At twenty-one, WG stood tall as a watch finisher while Hannah continued her work as a weaver. Their modest abode on Swanswell Terrace, a stone's throw from Tower Street and Chauntry Place, became their sanctuary as they navigated the joys and challenges of early marriage.

WG, sitting by the hearth in their modest home, the firelight casting flickering shadows on the walls, cradles Elizabeth in his arms, his voice tender as he speaks to Hannah. "Our little Lizzy, Hannah... who would've thought that one night could bring forth such a treasure? She's the light of our lives, the very proof of the love we dared to seize."

Hannah smiles softly, her hands busy with weaving, though her eyes are fixed on WG and their daughter. "Aye, Will, she is. But with that love came responsibilities, and we've not shied away from them. We made our vows before God and man, and now we build a life together, stone by stone."

WG, his gaze growing serious as he shifts Lizzy to a more comfortable position. "I've never doubted the path we chose, Hannah. Our union in Holy Trinity... It was more than just a duty. It was a promise—one I intend to keep, no matter the hardships we may face."

Hannah, her voice soft yet resolute, as she pauses in her work to look at him. "And face them we shall, together. There are whispers, Will, about us and our hurried marriage. But let them whisper. We've more strength than they know, and our love will see us through."

Nodding, his determination is evident as he gently rocks Elizabeth. "We've already proved our worth, haven't we? I've carved a place for myself as a watch finisher, and you, with your weaving... we've built this life with our own hands. Swanswell Terrace may be modest, but it's ours, and every inch of it tells our story."

With a smile that holds both pride and contentment, she resumes her weaving; her voice filled with quiet confidence. "And what a story it is. From the day you walked into the Golden Cross, I knew our lives would be intertwined. We've faced the world together, Will, and we'll continue to do so. For Lizzy's sake, for our own, we'll make this life the best it can be."

With a chuckle, he leans over to kiss Lizzy's forehead, then looks at Hannah with a grin. "And who knows? Perhaps one day, Lizzy will tell her own children about the love that built this home. A love forged in the heart of Coventry, under the shadow of Holy Trinity's spires."

Her voice is warm with affection as she nods, her eyes shining with love and determination. "A love that will endure, Will, as long as we keep faith in each other. This is just the beginning, and I look forward to every chapter we write together."

The fire crackles softly as they sit in companionable silence, each lost in their own thoughts yet profoundly connected by the life they are building. Outside, the city of Coventry hums with activity, but within the walls of Swanswell Terrace, there is only the quiet strength of a family determined to thrive.

Their union bore fruit with the arrival of Thomas in 1867, followed swiftly by Martha and another William in 1868.

Despite the growing family, WG's heart remained firmly tethered to Liverpool, where his roots ran deep. In Liverpool, his mother and father, the steadfast anchors of his early life, continued to reside. But more than that, his bond with his beloved half-sister Janie and younger sister Frances kept his spirit drawn back to the city.

Frances' birth had been a moment of joy amid the struggles of daily life, a new life that brought light to the Griffiths household. WG had felt a protective instinct over her, the same way he did with Janie. Despite the distance and his responsibilities in Coventry, thoughts of his sisters—one just beginning her journey through childhood, the other growing into a young woman—frequently occupied his mind. He imagined them playing in the streets of Liverpool, Janie guiding Frances with the same care and affection WG had shown her in their youth.

Every visit back to Liverpool was a balm to WG's weary soul, the sight of his family renewing his strength. Holding the infant Frances, WG felt a surge of emotions—pride, love, and a fierce determination to ensure a better future for her as well as his own children. He knew that despite the difficulties of his own life, he had to remain connected to them, to be the brother they could look up to, the one who would rise above the struggles they all faced.

As Frances grew, WG's bond with her deepened. He delighted in her curious nature and the way she looked up to him with wide, trusting eyes. Each time he returned to Liverpool, he saw the changes in her—how she began to toddle about, how her first words were spoken, and how she began to develop a personality all her own. Though fleeting, these moments reinforced WG's sense of duty, not just to his children in Coventry but to his family in Liverpool as well.

Liverpool was not just the city where he grew into a man; it was where his heart lay, where the ties of blood and love were strongest. No matter how far he travelled or how much his life changed, the connection to his family in Liverpool, especially to Janie and Frances, remained an unbreakable thread woven through the fabric of his existence.

The evening of February 27th 1870, began like any other for young Frances as she left Mrs. Thompson's house on Prescot Street, where she worked in service. At just twelve years old, Frances had grown accustomed to the short, solitary walk back to her home on Sparling Street. Though bustling by day, Liverpool's streets were eerily quiet as the shadows lengthened. The chill in the air caused her to pull her shawl tighter around her small frame as she quickened her pace, the familiar cobblestones clicking beneath her shoes.

As she turned onto Pembroke Place, Frances felt a prickle of unease creep up her spine. The street was unusually deserted, the usual sounds of laughter and chatter replaced by an unsettling silence. She glanced over her shoulder and caught sight of a figure—tall, shadowy, and too close for comfort—following her. The man's footsteps echoed hers, deliberate and steady, sending a wave of fear through her.

Her heart began to race, each beat loud in her ears as she tried to maintain her composure. She told herself it was nothing, that the man was just another passerby on his way home. But as she neared Catherine Street, the man quickened his pace, closing the distance between them. Panic set in, and Frances' breath came in short, sharp gasps.

In a moment of desperation, she darted into the narrow alley between two buildings, hoping to lose him in the maze of backstreets. But the man was relentless. He followed her into the alley, his hand reaching out to grab her. Frances yelped, twisting and turning, trying to free herself from his grasp.

"Where do you think you're going, little Miss?" the man sneered, his voice low and menacing as he tightened his hold on her arm.

"Let me go! Please, let me go!" Frances cried, her voice trembling with fear as she struggled against him, her tiny fists pounding helplessly on his chest.

The man's grip only tightened, his intentions becoming alarmingly clear as he pushed her against the brick wall and banged her head roughly. Dazed, Frances was not one to surrender easily. With all the strength she could muster, she kicked at his shins and bit down hard on his hand, causing him to yelp in pain and loosen his hold for just a moment.

Frances saw her chance and bolted, running as fast as her legs could carry her. She didn't dare look back; her only thought was to escape, to get away from the man who meant her harm. But she didn't get far before she felt his hand close around her wrist once more, yanking her back toward him. Just as she thought all hope was lost, a voice called out from the entrance to the alley.

"Get away from her, you filthy scoundrel!" A woman, older and sturdy, rushed toward them, brandishing a heavy umbrella like a weapon.

Startled, the man released Frances and turned to flee, disappearing into the night as quickly as he had appeared. The woman hurried to Frances' side, her face softening with concern as she took the trembling girl into her arms.

"There now, my dear. You're safe. He's gone," the woman soothed, her voice gentle as she wiped the tears from Frances' cheeks.

Frances clung to her saviour, her body shaking with sobs, the terror of the assault still fresh in her mind. The woman guided her back to the main road, her arm wrapped protectively around Frances' shoulders.

"What's your name, child? Where do you live?" the woman asked kindly, trying to distract Frances from the ordeal.

"Frances... Frances Griffiths. I live on Sparling Street," she managed to reply between sobs.

"Let's get you home, Frances. Your family will be worried sick."

The woman walked with her all the way to Sparling Street, her presence a comforting balm to Frances' frayed nerves. By the time they reached the Griffiths' front door, the shock of what had happened was beginning to take its toll. Frances thanked the woman, her voice barely more than a whisper, desperate to be enveloped in the warmth and safety of her home where Martha and William consoled her.

The sombre hues of twilight were cast as William and Martha Griffiths awaited the return of their young Frances. They had grown accustomed to the rhythmic, albeit solitary, returns of their twelve-year-old servant from Mrs. Thompson's house on Prescot Street. Yet, this evening promised to be unlike any other.

As the clock chimed eight, a timid knock upon the door startled them. William, a man with a keen sense of duty, opened it to reveal a woman of considerable stature and firm resolve, her breath visible in the cool evening air. Frances' trembling form was clasped in her strong hands, her face a portrait of raw, dishevelled distress.

"Your Frances," the woman began, her voice laden with the gravity of the night's events, "was beset upon by a vile assailant. I intervened just in time. She is safe now but deeply shaken."

As the woman recounted the harrowing events of the evening, William's face contorted with a mix of fear and rising fury. His hands, calloused from years of honest work, clenched into tight fists as he listened to the details of the assault. The shock of hearing what had nearly befallen his daughter was overwhelming, but anger quickly surged to the forefront, eclipsing his initial disbelief.

He stood and fixed the woman with a penetrating stare. "This scoundrel," he began, his voice low and seething with barely contained rage, "did you see him clear enough? What did he look like? I need to know, ma'am. Tell me everything you can remember about him."

The woman's eyes, filled with a mix of compassion and understanding, met William's. She hesitated for a brief moment, sensing the depth of his anguish. "He was tall," she said slowly, "and broad-shouldered, dressed in dark clothing that blended with the night. His face... it was shadowed, but I caught a glimpse when the moonlight hit him. He had a rough look about him, unshaven, with a scowl that could freeze the blood in your veins. His hair was dark, and his eyes... They were cold, cruel."

William's jaw tightened as he absorbed her words. "And his voice?" he pressed, "Did he speak to you or to Frances? Was there anything distinct about it?"

The woman nodded, recalling the chilling encounter. "He did speak, though only briefly. His voice was gruff, like gravel, and there was an edge of menace in his tone that made my skin crawl."

William's breath came in harsh, uneven bursts as he tried to contain his anger. "I'll find him," he vowed, his voice trembling with the weight of his promise. "No one lays a hand on my Frances and walks free. I'll see him brought to justice, I swear it."

Seeing the dangerous fire burning in her husband's eyes, Martha placed a gentle hand on his arm, trying to soothe his tempestuous spirit. "William, please," she urged softly, "think of Frances. She needs us here, now, more than anything. We'll leave this matter to the authorities, but tonight, our daughter needs to know that she is safe, that she is loved."

Though spoken with calm resolve, her words seemed to pierce through the fog of William's rage. He looked down at Frances, who was still trembling and felt a wave of guilt wash over him. His anger, though justified, would not help his daughter heal. He nodded slowly, forcing himself to focus on the immediate needs of his family.

"I will not rest," he said quietly, more to himself than anyone else, "until that man is found. But tonight, Martha, you're right. Tonight, we take care of Frances."

Her heart sinking, Martha grasped the woman's hands with fervent gratitude. "Oh, kind lady! We cannot thank you enough for your courage and compassion. Please, come in and let us offer you some refreshment if only to repay a fraction of the debt we owe."

The modest yet resolute woman accepted their invitation with a nod and stepped into the warm embrace of the Griffiths' modest parlour. William, a pillar of stoic strength, took a moment to absorb the harrowing news. His face, usually a mask of unruffled calm, now betrayed a mixture of disbelief and anguish.

"Such wretched cruelty," he murmured, shaking his head. "How fortunate we are that you arrived when you did. We are forever in your debt."

With a mutual nod, Martha guided the woman to a seat and hurried to fetch a pot of tea. As she worked, her mind was preoccupied with thoughts of Frances. The young girl had been through a terrible ordeal, and Martha's heart ached for her.

Meanwhile, William took Frances by the shoulders, his grip gentle yet firm. "Frances, my dear," he spoke softly, "you are safe now. We will see to your comfort and well-being."

Having settled into the warm surroundings, the woman began to recount the grim details of the night's events; her voice tinged with sorrow and indignation. She described how the shadowy figure that had pursued Frances, the confrontation in the alley, and her own intervention with the umbrella. Once the tale was told, Martha, having prepared a modest spread of bread and butter along with the tea, turned her attention entirely to Frances. She coaxed the frightened girl to a comfortable chair near the fire with utmost care. She wrapped Frances in a soft, woollen blanket and set about making her a warm, soothing drink.

The night wore on in a quiet, tender vigil. Though physically safe, except for a bruise on her temple, Frances was visibly shaken, her small frame trembling with residual fear. Martha and William tended to her with unwavering devotion, their actions a balm for the girl's emotional wounds. They spoke in hushed, comforting tones, their presence a steady anchor in the storm of Frances' mind.

As the warmth of the hearth and the comfort of Griffiths' care began to envelop her, Frances' sobs subsided, replaced by a fragile calm. The terror of the evening faded, if only slightly, as she nestled into the safety of her home, surrounded by those who had embraced her in her time of need.

With the night drawing to a close, the kind woman rose to leave, having fulfilled her noble duty. William and Martha expressed their heartfelt thanks once more, their words earnest and filled with deep appreciation. As the woman stepped out into the crisp night air, the Griffiths' household settled into a quiet, grateful repose, their hearts full of sorrow for the night's trials and immense gratitude for the kindness they had seen them through.

In the days that followed the assault, Frances tried to return to her regular routine, but the trauma of that night clung to her like a shadow. Her once bright eyes were now clouded with fear, and the laughter that had often echoed through the rooms of 42 Sparling Street was replaced with an unsettling silence. She tried to hide her bruises beneath her shawl, but the marks on her face betrayed the violence she had endured.

Her mother noticed the change immediately. Frances, usually so lively and cheerful, had become withdrawn and quiet, her once bright eyes now shadowed with a distant fear. Martha's heart ached at the sight, her motherly instincts flaring with concern. This wasn't the Frances she knew, the girl who once laughed freely and danced around their small home, the very essence of innocence and joy. Something terrible had happened.

When questioned, Frances spoke little of the incident, her voice a fragile whisper that barely escaped her lips. She avoided her mother's eyes, her small hands trembling as they clutched the hem of her dress. It was as if speaking of the ordeal would somehow make it more real, more terrifying. Perhaps, in her young mind, she thought that she could protect her family from the horrors she had faced by keeping silent. But the signs were there, etched into the very fabric of her being—a shudder at the slightest sound, the way she recoiled from shadows that seemed to loom more prominent than before, and the tears that came unbidden in the quiet of the night.

Martha, however, was not so easily appeased. The anguish in her daughter's eyes mirrored a pain she knew all too well, one that had haunted her for years. She pressed Frances for details, her voice firm but laced with the softness of a mother's love, urging her to share the burden she carried. "Frances, my love, please tell me what happened," Martha whispered, her hands gently cupping the girl's face, forcing her to meet her gaze. "You mustn't keep this inside. I need to know so I can help you."

Frances hesitated, her eyes welling with tears. She bit her lip, torn between fear and the need to unburden herself. Finally, she spoke, her words tumbling out in a rush of pain and confusion. She told Martha about the man, the shadowy figure who had appeared out of nowhere as she made her way home. He had grabbed her, his grip like iron, as he dragged her into the darkened alley. The smell of his breath, rancid and hot against her cheek, was something she would never forget.

"He said terrible things, Mama," Frances choked out, her small body trembling as she relived the nightmare. "He... he tried to hurt me, but the lady... she saved me. She hit him with her umbrella, and I ran."

Martha listened, her heart breaking with each word. The terror in Frances' voice transported her back to a time when she had been the one cornered, vulnerable and alone. Martha's own memories of that dark day surged to the forefront of her mind, unbidden and unwelcome. She had been just a girl, much like Frances, walking home from when she had been assaulted. Her attacker had been a nameless, faceless monster, preying on the innocent with no remorse. She had fought back with everything she had, her screams echoing, but no one had come to her aid. By the time he fled, Martha was left bruised and broken, her spirit shattered. The aftermath had been unbearable—the whispers, the shame, the feeling that she had been forever tainted by what had happened.

She had vowed then and there that she would never let anyone hurt her like that again. But now, hearing Frances' account, it was as if history was repeating itself, and the wounds she thought had healed long ago were ripped open once more.

Martha pulled Frances into her arms, holding her close as the girl sobbed into her shoulder. "Oh, my darling," she murmured, her voice thick with emotion. "I'm so sorry. I'm so sorry this happened to you."

Frances clung to her mother, the safety of her embrace a balm to her frayed nerves. "I was so scared, Mama. I didn't know what to do."

"You did everything right, Frances," Martha reassured her, stroking her hair. "You fought back, and you got away. You're safe now, and that's what matters. No one will ever hurt you again; I promise you that."

As Martha held her daughter, she felt a renewed sense of determination. She wouldn't let Frances carry the same burden she had carried all these years. She would be there for her, to guide her through the pain, to help her heal. No one should have to face such darkness alone, and Martha would make sure that Frances never would. The scars from Martha's own assault had never truly faded, but perhaps in helping her daughter through this, she could begin to heal the wounds that had been festering in her own heart for far too long.

Frances continued to assure her mother that she was fine, that the bruises would heal, and that she just needed a bit of rest. But the physical and emotional toll of the assault was far greater than anyone could have imagined. Over the next few days, Frances grew increasingly pale and weak. She complained of headaches that throbbed incessantly, of a burning thirst that no amount of water could quench. Her mother watched helplessly as her daughter's condition worsened, her heart breaking as Frances' once-rosy cheeks turned an alarming shade of grey.

Then, one night, the terror of that dark alley seemed to revisit Frances in her sleep. She awoke with a start, her body convulsing in violent fits. Her cries echoed through the small house, rousing her family from their beds. They rushed to her side, but there was little they could do but watch in horror as Frances writhed in pain, her small frame no match for the illness that had taken hold.

As dawn broke, Frances lay still, her breath shallow and laboured. The fits had passed, but they had left her utterly drained. A surgeon was called, and he arrived swiftly, but despite his best efforts, it was clear that Frances was slipping away. He examined her carefully, noting the bruises on her temples and the paleness of her skin. His brow furrowed as he considered her symptoms, but he found no apparent connection between the assault and her current state. After a long pause, he declared that she was suffering from blood poisoning, likely brought on by typhus fever, a common but deadly illness in the crowded streets of Liverpool.

Martha listened in stunned silence as the surgeon delivered his prognosis. The words seemed hollow as if they belonged to someone else, but the truth was undeniable. Frances' life was ebbing away before her eyes. The surgeon prescribed what little he could to ease her pain, but as the hours passed, it became apparent that nothing would save the young girl.

Martha wringing her hands, her voice trembling as she spoke to William. "She's been so quiet these past few days, Will... too quiet. Ever since that dreadful night, it's as though the light's gone out of her eyes."

His brow furrowed, he stared into the fire, the flames reflecting in his dark eyes as he clenched his fists. "I should have collected her from Mrs. Thompson's. I should've been there... to protect her from that vile scoundrel. If I ever lay my hands on him..."

Interrupting, her voice choked with tears. "What good would it do now, Will? The damage is done. Our poor Frances... she's been so strong, but it's as though something's eating away at her from within."

Suddenly, a faint cry came from the room above, followed by the sound of thrashing. Martha shot to her feet, her face pale with fear.

Martha's voice frantic, "Will, she's taken another fit! We must go to her!"

They hurried up the narrow staircase, the sound of Frances's pained moans growing louder with each step. When they reached her room, they found her tossing and turning in her bed, her face flushed with fever and her tiny body drenched in sweat.

Frances, whimpering, her voice weak and tremulous, "Mum... Dad... it hurts... make it stop..."

Martha rushed to her side, smoothing her daughter's damp hair from her forehead, her heart breaking at the sight of her child's suffering.

Soothingly, though her own voice shook with fear. "Hush now, my sweet girl... we're here with you. Everything will be alright."

William stood helplessly at the foot of the bed, his hands trembling as he watched his daughter writhing in pain. He had faced many hardships in his life, but nothing had prepared him for this—a helplessness that gnawed at his soul, knowing that he could do nothing to ease his daughter's suffering.

His voice was thick with emotion. "I should fetch the doctor again... perhaps there's something more he can do for her."

Martha shook her head, her voice barely a whisper. "The doctor said there's nothing more to be done, Will. She... she's slipping away from us."

Frances cried out again, her small hand clutching her mother's desperately. Her voice was faint, barely more than a breath. "Mum... I'm scared... don't let go..."

Holding her tightly, tears streaming down her cheeks. "I'm right here, my darling... I won't let go, I promise."

The night wore on, each hour seeming longer than the last as Frances's fever raged on. As dawn approached, her strength began to fade, and her breath came in ragged gasps.

Frances, her voice barely audible, her eyes fluttering closed. "Mum... Dad... I'm so tired..."

William's voice cracked as he knelt beside the bed, taking her other hand in his. "Rest now, my sweet girl... rest and know that we love you... always."

With one final, shuddering breath, Frances fell still, her small hand slipping from her mother's grasp. A silence fell over the room, broken only by the sound of Martha's sobs as she clutched her daughter's lifeless body to her chest.

Martha, her voice a broken whisper, her tears falling onto Frances's pale face. "My baby... my sweet Frances..."

William stood motionless, his heart shattered, as he stared down at the lifeless form of his daughter. The room seemed to close in around him, the walls pressing in as the reality of what had happened settled over him like a suffocating weight. He had lost his little girl, and no amount of anger, no thirst for vengeance, could bring her back.

William, his voice hollow, his gaze distant. "She was too young, Martha... too young to be taken from us."

Nodding through her tears, her voice a broken sob. "She was... and it's all my fault. I should have never let her go out alone that night."

William, his voice barely more than a whisper, his eyes filled with sorrow. "We did what we thought was best, Martha... but the world is cruel, and it's taken our Frances from us."

As the first light of day crept into the room, William and Martha held each other close, their hearts united in grief, as they mourned the loss of their beloved daughter. The world outside continued to turn, oblivious to their pain, as life in Liverpool carried on as it always had. But for William and Martha, nothing would ever be the same again.

Frances's tragic demise in 1870, while still so young and toiling in service at Mrs. Thompson's house on Prescot Street, struck Griffiths' world with a force that shattered their every hope. The brutal assault she had endured and the subsequent death from blood poisoning left her parents, William and Martha Griffiths, utterly devastated. The heartbreak of losing their beloved daughter was a wound that would not heal, searing through their hearts with relentless agony.

William and Martha, once vibrant and full of life, were consumed by their grief. The pain of their loss seemed to sap the very strength from their souls, leaving them shadowed and broken.

In a desperate attempt to escape the relentless reminders of their loss, William and Martha decided to leave Liverpool. They sought refuge with WG and his wife, Hannah, in Albert Street, Coventry, hoping that a change of environment might lift the shroud of despair that had enveloped their lives and believing that the warmth of family might offer them solace.

Yet, the anguish and grief that had gripped them proved insurmountable. The physical distance from their former home in Liverpool did little to alleviate the emotional pain that plagued them. Though geographically distant, the new surroundings could not dispel the heavy cloud of mourning that followed them.

Within the year of their move, the overwhelming weight of their grief took its final toll. William, whose heart had been shattered by the loss of his daughter, found himself descending into a sorrow that gnawed at his very soul. The once vigorous man, known for his strength and resolve, was now a shadow of his former self. Grief took root deep within him, and his health, once robust, began to fail. The weight of his sorrow grew heavier each day, his heart no longer able to bear the burden of such profound loss.

His steps grew slower, his breaths more laboured, as if each one was an effort to keep a grasp on the life that was slipping through his fingers. The light in his eyes dimmed, replaced by a haunting emptiness that no comfort could fill. It was as though the life had been drained from him, and one fateful evening, as the sun dipped below the horizon, William's heart, fragile and worn, finally gave out. He passed quietly in his sleep, the pain of his grief easing only in death, leaving behind the memory of a man who had loved deeply and lost more than he could bear.

Martha, a woman once brimming with warmth and vitality, found herself even adrift in a sea of sorrow after the devastating loss of her beautiful Frances and beloved companion, William. The grief that settled over her was profound, an unshakable shadow that clung to her every waking moment. She wandered through the days in a daze, her once bright spirit dulled by the heavy weight of her despair.

Martha's heart, already fragile from the passing of her daughter, could not withstand the added blow of William's death. She became a ghost of her former self, her steps slower, her voice softer, as though speaking too loudly might shatter what little remained of her strength.

Her health, which had always been sturdy, began to falter under the strain of her grief. The vibrancy in her eyes faded, replaced by a deep, abiding sadness that no comfort could alleviate. She took to her bed, the weight of her sorrow too great to bear upright. Family came to sit with her, to offer what solace they could, but it was as though Martha had already begun her journey to join those she had loved so dearly.

A few months after William's passing, Martha took her final breath on a quiet, chilly morning. Her face, once etched with lines of worry and pain, softened in death as if she had finally found the peace that had eluded her in life. She passed gently, like a candle extinguished by a soft breeze, her heart finally at rest, reunited with her beloved Frances and William in whatever lay beyond this world.

Thus, both William and Martha Griffiths, bound together in life and in grief, passed away within the same year, leaving

WG and Hannah to witness the tragic culmination of a family's suffering. The house on Albert Street, once a beacon of hope for a new beginning, now stood as a silent testament to the depth of their sorrow and the unrelenting shadow that had claimed them all.

The tragic events that befell WG weighed heavily upon him, casting a dark pall over his life. The loss of his sister, Frances, under such harrowing circumstances had already shattered the delicate balance of his world. The grief of losing his parents, who had come to live under his roof only to pass away within a year, deepened the burden he carried.

The weight of these sorrows took a considerable toll on his marriage to Hannah. The once vibrant union now found itself strained by the unrelenting pressures of personal loss and economic hardship. The strain of maintaining the household while grappling with such profound grief led to frequent discord, overshadowing the love that had once been the foundation of their relationship.

Within a few years, the arrival of Richard marked a new beginning, a birth of hope amid the shadows of grief that had enveloped WG since the tragic loss of his parents and sister, Frances. The day felt like a bittersweet reprieve, with joy and sorrow intertwined in an intricate dance. The shadows of despair still loomed heavy over him, each memory a sharp reminder of the pain that had carved deep lines into his heart.

Yet, as he held the small boy in his arms, a flicker of light pierced the darkness, warming the cold corners of his sorrow.

Richard, with his wide eyes and innocent laughter, seemed to radiate a joy that was foreign to WG in that moment. The boy's presence was a reminder of hope, a new beginning amidst the chaos of loss. As Richard giggled, his spirit unburdened by the weight of grief, WG felt a gentle nudge from the universe—a sign that, even in the depths of despair, life could still offer moments of light and love. It was a brief but precious reminder that amid heartache, there could still be beauty, a chance to nurture and protect the next generation, and perhaps, to heal in the process.

For respite from the grief, WG would spar with the local men at the newly established sporting club at The Butts. Boxing, once merely a passion for WG, evolved into something far more significant—it became his refuge from the overwhelming grief and emotional turmoil that had accumulated over the years. The physicality of the ring allowed him to channel his frustrations and sorrow into something tangible, offering brief moments of relief from the emotional burden he carried. After the deaths of his parents and the loss of his beloved sister, Frances, boxing became a way to cope, a controlled outlet where he could feel in control when everything else in life seemed to slip away.

What began as a personal release soon turned into a means of survival. Facing mounting financial pressures, WG entered the world of prizefighting, where his boxing skills could earn him money—though the income was often erratic and insufficient. The fights provided an escape, but they also led him down a dangerous path. As the stakes grew, so did the toll on his body and his spirit. Prizefighting became a double-edged sword, offering both fleeting financial relief and deeper bruises, both physical and emotional.

However, WG's involvement in the underground world of boxing came with consequences. His brushes with the law increased, as his reputation for violence inside and outside the ring began to spread. The tension from his financial struggles, coupled with his increasingly troubled reputation, began to strain his marriage. The very thing that had initially helped him cope with his grief now created friction in his personal life, eroding the trust and stability in his marriage, leaving WG in a constant battle with his inner demons.

WG's frequent legal troubles and increasingly erratic behaviour cast a shadow over his once-reputable name. The very skills that had promised him a measure of financial relief became a source of further turmoil, exacerbating the strain on his relationship with Hannah. Their home, which had once been a refuge from the world's troubles, now echoed with the discord of unresolved grief and mounting frustration.

As WG's struggles deepened, his path became increasingly fraught with difficulty. The emotional and financial burdens and his growing disillusionment led him down a darker road. His life, once full of potential and hope, now seemed to spiral into a series of misfortunes and missteps, leaving him grappling with the remnants of his shattered dreams and the persistent shadows of his past.

In 1874, when the gavel fell and the word "guilty" echoed through the courtroom, WG felt his world tilt sharply on its axis. The fraud charge, brought on by a desperate attempt to provide for his family, landed him in prison—a place where his past as a prizefighter became both a shield and a curse.

"You're a fighter, ain't ya?" one of the older inmates asked him on his first day, eyeing WG's broad shoulders and the hardened look in his eyes.

"Used to be," WG replied tersely, not eager to advertise his skills but knowing it was futile to deny. But that was a long time ago," in an attempt to disguise the present.

"Don't matter how long it's been," the inmate said with a knowing smirk. "In here, you'll need those fists more than ever."

And he was right. WG quickly found that his reputation preceded him. While his pugilistic talents kept some of the more dangerous inmates at bay, they also drew unwanted attention. Every few weeks, someone would challenge him, eager to make a name for themselves by taking down the once-great fighter.

"You think you're still tough, Griffiths?" a fellow prisoner sneered during one of these inevitable confrontations.

WG didn't answer with words. His fists spoke for him, landing blows that echoed off the prison's stone walls. Each fight was a reminder of what he had been but also of how far he had fallen.

In 1877, after his release, WG knew he couldn't easily return to the life he'd left behind. The weight of his failures and the shame of his imprisonment kept him from going home. Instead, he sought a different path that took him far from the familiar streets of Coventry and deep into the nomadic world of a travelling circus.

"Shiny's what they call me," WG said with a grim smile to the circus ringleader, who asked him about his past. "Not just for the fights I win, but for the shoes I mend. I picked up cobbling in prison—it gave me something to do with my hands other than throwing punches."

The ringleader, a wiry man with a flair for the dramatic, looked him up and down. "A fighter who can fix shoes, eh? That's a first. You'll fit in just fine here, Shiny."

WG found a strange sort of peace among the circus folk. The life was rough, but it was honest in a way that his old life had never been. He fought when he had to—prizefighting for the amusement of the crowds—but he also mended shoes for his fellow travellers, taking pride in his work and the new identity he had carved out for himself.

But by 1879, the winds of change blew through his life once again, proving that peace was a fleeting thing for a man like

WG. The circus, which had become his refuge, was no longer enough to fill the void inside him. The constant movement, endless fights, and solitary nights began to wear him down.

"I can't keep running, not from this, not from myself," WG muttered to himself one night as he stared into the campfire, his hands absently polishing a worn pair of boots. "It's time to face what I've been avoiding."

With that realisation, WG knew that another tumultuous turn in his life was inevitable. The question was no longer about whether he would change course but when and how. And so, with the name "Shiny" echoing in his ears, he began to plan his next move—one that would bring him full circle, back to the life he had tried so hard to escape.

Tom Green

Born in the bustling Lancashire town of Prescot, Liverpool in 1840, Tom Green entered the world amidst the cacophony of his parent's butcher shop. His father, a stoic man of few words, and his mother, a bustling figure perpetually surrounded by the aroma of meat and the chatter of customers, instilled in Tom and his elder brother Richard (known affectionately as 'Dickie') a sense of hard work and determination from an early age.

The Green boys were inseparable; their childhood was a tapestry woven with mischief and dreams. While their parents toiled in the shop, Tom and Richard often slipped away to explore the nooks and crannies of Prescot. During one of these escapades, they stumbled upon Thomas Byron's workshop—a haven of ticking timepieces and delicate mechanisms that immediately captivated their imaginations.

Thomas Byron, a skilled watchmaker of repute in Prescot, took the young boys under his wing. He saw in them a raw talent for precision and a hunger for knowledge that mirrored his youthful ambitions. Under his tutelage, Tom flourished as an apprentice, his nimble fingers deftly handling delicate gears and intricacies of watchmaking. It was here, amidst the comforting tick-tock of clocks and the aroma of oiled metal, that Tom forged a path he had scarcely imagined.

The workshop became a sanctuary for the Green brothers and their newfound friend, WG. A few years younger than Tom and Dickie, WG possessed a quiet strength and a steely resolve that drew the elder boys to him like moths to a flame. Together, they navigated the winding streets of Prescot, their boyhood days punctuated by escapades that often led them to the makeshift camps of Irish settlers on Kemble Street and Hillock Street.

In these rough-and-tumble neighbourhoods, where poverty and resilience coexisted in equal measure, WG discovered an unexpected talent for boxing.

On a chilly evening, WG's first opportunity to fight presented itself by chance, as many things did in those days. WG, Tom, and Dickie were loitering near Hillock Street when they noticed a makeshift ring being set up in a muddy square. A crowd had begun to gather, eager for the evening's entertainment.

Ever the instigator, Tom nudged WG, pointing out a traveller boy boasting about being unbeaten and challenging anyone to face him. Despite initial doubts, WG was drawn in by the thrill of the challenge. Dickie, sensing WG's hesitation, highlighted the potential for earning money through bets.

Determined, WG agreed to fight. The bout began with the traveller boy launching a powerful onslaught, but WG, lighter on his feet, dodged and waited for the right moment. As the boy grew frustrated, WG seized the opportunity, landing quick, precise jabs that surprised the crowd and ultimately won the fight with a final uppercut.

The victory was more than just a test of strength for WG; it was a glimpse of a future where he could rise above the hardships of their world, one punch at a time. With Tom and Dickie by his side, WG found a new purpose in the makeshift rings, his ambition to excel and overcome their humble beginnings growing stronger with each fight.

As the years unfolded, so did the bonds between the three friends. Their discussions often turned to the elusive promise of wealth and opportunity beyond Lancashire's borders. With memories of his birthplace near Coventry haunting his dreams, WG frequently spoke of the possibilities awaiting them in the industrial heartlands of England. Tom, meanwhile, found himself captivated not just by the intricacies of watchmaking but by the enchanting Jane Byron—the spirited daughter of his mentor.

Jane Byron, a vision of grace amidst the clangour of her father's workshop, captured Tom's heart with a fierceness that mirrored his ambitions. Their courtship blossomed amidst the ticking of clocks and the scent of oil, culminating in a union that raised eyebrows among the Byron family. Tom, ever the determined suitor, won over Jane's father with a blend of charm and unwavering dedication, and in 1862, they exchanged vows at St. Wilfrid's in Farnworth.

Married life brought its own set of challenges and joys for Tom and Jane. The birth of their first child, James, heralded a new chapter filled with the cacophony of children's laughter and the responsibilities of parenthood. Meanwhile, Dickie followed in his brother's footsteps, finding love with Jane's elder sister, Elizabeth. Once wary of Tom's adventurous spirit, the Byron and Green families found themselves united by the bonds of marriage and shared dreams.

Amidst the changing fortunes of the time, Dickie found himself increasingly disillusioned with the watchmaking trade in Prescot. The once-thriving industry, which had sustained families for generations, was now plagued by uncertainty. The passage of the Truck Act had sent ripples through the local economy, tightening the grip of hardship on artisans who had long relied on the trade. Payments in goods instead of currency became common, making it difficult to make ends meet, even for the most skilled craftsmen.

Seeing the writing on the wall, Dickie began to question whether a future in watchmaking could truly provide the security and prosperity he desired. Conversations with fellow workers often turned to the opportunities beyond Prescot—tales of burgeoning industries in other cities, where men could make a decent living without the yoke of outdated practices dragging them down.

It was during one of these late-night discussions at the local tavern, with a pint of ale in hand and the fire crackling in the hearth, that Dickie made his decision. With its flourishing small arms industry, Birmingham offered the promise of a new career as a barrel turner—a trade rapidly growing in demand. The city's reputation as the "workshop of the world" was hard to ignore, and Dickie saw in it a chance to escape the diminishing returns of watchmaking and build a better life for himself and Elizabeth.

With a heavy heart, he shared his decision with Tom. "I've been thinkin', Tom," he said one evening as they sat by the window overlooking the dimly lit streets of Prescot. "This town's been good to us, but the times are changin'. The work's gettin' harder, and the pay's just not enough. I've heard good things about Birmingham—about the small arms trade. They say a man can make a real go of it there, turnin' barrels and the like."

Tom listened, his own thoughts mirroring Dickie's concerns. The pressures of providing for their growing families were all too familiar. Though he would miss his brother's presence, Tom understood that Dickie's decision was driven by the same desire for security that kept him awake at night, pondering the uncertain future that lay ahead.

And so, with a mix of apprehension and resolve, Dickie prepared to leave the familiar streets of Prescot behind, setting his sights on Birmingham, where a new chapter awaited.

As time passed, beneath the surface of domestic bliss, the strains of providing for a growing family began to weigh heavily on Tom's shoulders. The demands of watchmaking, once a source of pride and purpose, now became a relentless pursuit of stability in an ever-changing world. Tom's letters with Dickie in Birmingham and WG in Coventry spoke of financial pressures and the irresistible allure of new beginnings in the bustling cityscapes beyond Prescot.

Over the years, the weight of raising a large family pressed heavily on Tom Green's shoulders. His home in Prescot was a constant bustle of activity with the cries of newborns and the boisterous laughter of growing children. Jane, his steadfast partner, managed the household with resilience as they welcomed their six children: Alice, James, Richard, Ann, William and Tom. Each child brought their own joys and challenges, and managing a household of this size was both a blessing and a burden.

The demands of watchmaking in Prescot, once a reliable source of income, became increasingly strained. Economic shifts and industry challenges made it difficult to maintain financial stability. Tom's letters reflected his growing concerns about their future, revealing his longing for a more secure opportunity.

WG's letters had arrived from Coventry with a steady rhythm, each one carrying tales of opportunity and the promise of a better life. With its burgeoning industries and expanding markets, the bustling city seemed to WG a place where ambition could finally meet with success. He spoke of the watchmaking trade, which, though still challenging, was growing in Coventry. WG himself had carved out a modest but growing reputation; his skills honed through persistence and sheer determination. In one of these letters, he first floated the idea to Tom—a suggestion that he might consider bringing his talents to Coventry, where a fresh start might bring new prosperity.

"Tom," WG wrote, his words filled with the earnestness of a brother who had found a foothold in uncertain times, "there's work here and good work at that. The city's growing, and with it, the demand for skilled hands like yours. If you're willin' to make the move, I've no doubt you'd do well here. We could even set up a small shop together—two brothers, side by side, just like old times."

The idea took root in Tom's mind, growing more appealing with each passing day. The struggles in Liverpool and the Truck Act had worn on him, and the thought of a new beginning where he might work alongside WG brought a glimmer of hope. But the move was not without its difficulties. Tom knew that starting anew in Coventry would require funds—more than he had saved. He would need to establish himself, acquire tools, and secure a place to live.

With a heavy heart, Tom approached Jane's father, Mr. Byron, a man of modest means but generous spirit. Tom laid out his hopes and plans over a cup of tea in the small parlour of the Byron household. "Mr. Byron," he began, carefully choosing his words, "I've been thinkin' of movin' to Coventry. WG's doin' well there, and he's asked me to join him. But... I'll need some help to get started—a loan if you'd be willin'. I'd repay every penny, of course, once I'm on my feet."

Mr. Byron, though cautious, saw the determination in Tom's eyes, and after a moment of thought, he nodded. "You're a hard worker, Tom, and you've always been good to Jane. I'll help you, but you must promise me that you'll take care of my daughter and your little ones. Coventry's a far cry from Liverpool, and it won't be easy."

Tom agreed, his heart filled with gratitude and resolve. But the decision brought with it another burden—the knowledge that Jane would remain behind in Liverpool with the support of her parents, at least for a time, until he created a sustainable home for his family. They had discussed it at length, weighing the benefits and risks. Jane's family was in Liverpool; they could offer her the support she would need while Tom found his footing in Coventry. It was a difficult choice, but they both understood that it was the best way forward for their growing family.

And so, with a mixture of hope and trepidation, Tom set his sights on Coventry, leaving Jane and their young family in the care of her family. The separation would be hard, but they knew it was a sacrifice worth making for the future they envisioned—a future where they would be reunited in a place that held the promise of prosperity and a new beginning.

From the moment WG set his sights on Coventry, Tom could sense a change in him. With its busy railway station bringing new settlers to the thriving city with winding streets, the city seemed to pull WG in, promising a better life but concealing its darker side. WG had always been ambitious, but Coventry awakened a hunger in him that Tom had seen before—but now witnessed first-hand. WG seemed to chase after something elusive. Coventry, at that time, stood at the heart of the watchmaking industry, known far and wide as the centre of the craft. Wealth and opportunity were evident in the city's thriving workshops and guilds. However, success in this prestigious trade was hard-earned, requiring both skill and perseverance. Money flowed through the city's watchmaking quarters, but only for those who could master the intricate art and keep pace with the industry's high standards. Tom noticed that WG was increasingly relying on prizefighting to make ends meet. Boxing had once been little more than a pastime for WG, an occasional escape from his daily routines. But after the devastating loss of both his parents and his beloved younger sister, Frances, the sport took on a deeper, more desperate meaning. What was once a hobby had become a refuge, a way to numb the pain and fill the void their absence left behind. The winnings from those brutal fights became essential, transforming into a lifeline that helped him support Hannah and provide the life she envisioned for their children. Yet, the cost was steep.

Each victory in the ring came at a price, chipping away at him both physically and morally. The bruises, broken bones, and the weight of compromise wore him down, even as the money kept coming. Tom, ever watchful, noticed how WG spoke of the winnings as though they were his last lifeline, clinging to them with a sense of desperation that hinted at something more. It was as if the memory of their parents and Frances weighed on him, with each fight a battle not just for survival, but for something lost—something that could never be reclaimed.

Hannah wasn't oblivious to it, either. She longed for more than what WG could offer, even with the prizefighting income. She wanted stability, a proper home, and a future for her children. Instead, she got a husband who was more absent than present, leaving her to fend for herself while he chased after fleeting glory with a travelling circus. WG had joined one of those circuses, fighting in makeshift rings for crowds who cared more about seeing blood than about who won or lost. With every fight, he drifted further away, leaving Hannah alone with her disappointments.

During WG's long absences, Tom began to take more notice of Hannah's situation. At first, checking in on her while WG was away was out of a sense of duty. But over time, Tom saw how much WG's choices were straining their marriage. Hannah was struggling, not just with loneliness, but with the uncertainty of what WG would be like when he returned—if he returned at all. Their conversations grew more frequent, and what began as friendly concern gradually deepened into something more. They found comfort in each other, a brief escape from their burdens.

Tom's trips to see Hannah had become more frequent, each visit a little longer than the last and each goodbye more difficult. The tension between them grew unspoken but undeniable. On a late autumn evening, the air crisp and the sun dipping below the horizon, their relationship finally crossed the line; they had both been tiptoeing around for months.

Tom had stopped by Hannah's small cottage to check on her, as he had often done since WG's departure with the circus. She greeted him at the door, her eyes shadowed with worry but brightening at the sight of him.

"Tom, it's good to see you," she said, her voice warm but tinged with weariness. "The house feels so empty when you're not around."

Tom stepped inside, noticing how cold the house had become without a steady fire burning. He took her hand, a gesture meant to comfort, but something in the way their fingers lingered told them both this visit would be different.

"Hannah," Tom began, his voice faltering as he looked into her eyes. "I don't know how to say this, but I can't keep pretending that I don't feel... something more for you. With WG being like my brother, I know it's wrong, but... you deserve better than the life he's giving you."

Hannah looked away, her eyes filling with unshed tears. "Tom, I've been so lonely. I've tried to be strong for the children and for myself, but WG... he's gone more than he's here, and when he is, it's like he's somewhere else entirely. I don't know who he is anymore."

Tom pulled her close, their bodies brushing as the fire crackled softly in the background. The distance between them, once a respectful barrier, was now charged with an undeniable need. They stood there for a moment, the weight of their unspoken desires pressing down on them until the silence was too heavy to bear.

"Hannah," Tom whispered, his breath warm against her skin. "If you want me to leave, just say the word, and I'll go. But if you don't..."

Hannah didn't reply with words. Instead, she reached up, cupping his face with her hands, and kissed him softly, tentatively at first. Tom hesitated for just a moment, but then as if a dam had broken, he kissed her back, the tenderness quickly giving way to a desperation that had been building between them for too long.

They moved together, wordlessly now, guided by an instinctual understanding of what they both needed. Tom's hands trembled as he undid the buttons on her dress, his breath hitching as he felt her skin beneath his fingers. Hannah's heart pounded as she led him to the small bed tucked away in the corner of the room, their shared guilt drowned out by the overwhelming desire that had taken hold of them.

As they lay together in the dim light, the final barriers between them fell away, and they gave in to the passion that had been simmering for so long. Their movements were hurried, almost frantic, as if they both knew this was a point of no return, yet neither could stop themselves.

Afterwards, as they lay tangled in each other's arms, the reality of what they had done began to settle in. Tom's fingers traced idle patterns on Hannah's bare shoulder, his mind a whirl of conflicting emotions.

"We can't be doing this again", he murmured, though even as he said it, he knew it would be impossible to resist the pull that had brought them together.

"I know," Hannah replied, her voice barely a whisper. "But what else is there for us? WG's not coming back, not really. And I can't keep pretending that everything's fine when it's not."

Tom sighed deeply, knowing that their lives had become irrevocably intertwined, their futures now uncertain and fraught with risk. "I don't have the answers, Hannah. But I do know that I care about you more than I should. And I'll do what I can to make this right... whatever that means."

As they drifted off to sleep, the fire's flickering light casting soft shadows on the walls, they both understood that this was just the beginning of something they couldn't easily escape—something that would change their lives forever.

Tom knew what they were doing was wrong. Guilt gnawed at him every time he was with Hannah, reminding him of Jane and the children back in Liverpool. He still made the occasional trip back to see them, trying to maintain the role of a devoted husband and father. But each time he returned, it became harder to leave Hannah behind. She was everything Jane wasn't—present, understanding, and in need of someone.

Yet, even as their affair deepened, Tom couldn't shake the feeling that they were both on a path with no return. WG was out there somewhere, fighting for a life that was slipping through his fingers, while Tom was betraying him in the worst possible way. But in those stolen moments with Hannah, all Tom could think about was how to keep the guilt at bay, if only for a little while longer.

As WG strode through the familiar streets of Coventry, his once-proud figure now cloaked in the weariness of the road, he couldn't shake the feeling that something was amiss. With every match and every fight under the circus tent, "Shiny" became synonymous with grit and resilience. His ability to adapt gained him the admiration of both the performers and the crowds. His reputation grew as someone who could weather hardship, with his gleaming shoes becoming a signature of sorts—a symbol of the battles he'd fought and survived, both inside the ring and in life. To those who travelled with him, "Shiny" came to represent WG's unyielding spirit, shining through the hardships he had endured.

The name seemed to take on a life of its own, evolving into something legendary. Stories about "Shiny" circulated throughout the circus world, with each telling adding another layer to his mystique. He wasn't just a cobbler or a fighter anymore—he was a symbol of perseverance, someone who had taken the blows of life and emerged from them, polished and ready for more.

But the glamour of the circus life had worn thin, and the echoes of his past had called him back home. He had left to make a name for himself, to find glory in the ring, but now, as he approached the humble dwelling he had once shared with Hannah, dread gnawed at him.

His heart sank as he reached the doorstep, finding it eerily silent. The usual sounds of life—Hannah bustling about or the faint murmur of conversations—were absent. Instead, he was greeted by a cold, empty space. WG pushed open the door, his pulse quickening as he stepped inside, the emptiness of the room reflecting the emptiness he felt within.

A neighbour, Mrs. Collins, appeared at the threshold, her expression a mix of pity and disapproval. "She's gone, you know," she said, her voice low but firm.

"Where?" WG demanded, his voice rough from weeks on the road.

"The workhouse. She had no choice—couldn't manage on her own after you left," Mrs Collins replied. She hesitated, then added, "Her father's there too, you know. And... she's with child."

WG's heart stopped. "With child?" he echoed, barely believing what he was hearing.

Mrs Collins nodded, her eyes narrowing. "She says it's Tom's. She's been carrying on with him while you were away."

The news hit WG like a punch to the gut. His fists clenched, the anger rising within him. "Tom? That scoundrel!" WG spat, his voice trembling with fury. "Where is he now?"

"Back in Liverpool, with his wife and family," Mrs Collins replied, her tone laced with judgement. "Seems he's unaware of the mess he's left behind here."

WG stood frozen, his mind racing. The betrayal, the abandonment, the shame—it all came crashing down on him. His first instinct was to confront Tom, to demand answers, to reclaim his honour. But as the initial shock began to fade, a cold, calculating resolve took its place.

WG's footsteps echoed ominously as he approached the workhouse gates, the grim facade casting long shadows in the fading light. His heart pounded with a mix of anger and dread as he entered, the stench of despair hanging heavy in the air. He had to see her—to hear the truth from her lips.

The matron, a stern woman with a no-nonsense air, led him down a narrow corridor lined with worn wooden doors. "She's in there," the matron said curtly, pointing to a room at the end. WG nodded in thanks, his jaw set as he approached.

Pushing open the door, WG found Hannah sitting on a narrow cot, her hands resting on her swollen belly. The sight of her, visibly pregnant, sent a fresh wave of fury coursing through him. She looked up, her eyes widening in surprise and fear as she saw him.

"Will..." she began, her voice trembling.

"Don't you 'Will' me," he snapped, stepping into the room and slamming the door behind him. "How could you? How could you do this to me? To us?"

Hannah looked down, her hands nervously fidgeting. "I didn't want it to happen this way," she whispered. "You left. You left me alone with nothing. What was I supposed to do?"

"Alone? Nothing?" WG scoffed, his voice rising with each word. "I left to make something of myself for you, for the children! And this is how you repay me? By lying with another man—Tom, no less!"

Tears welled up in Hannah's eyes as she looked up at him, her voice thick with emotion. "I was desperate. Tom was here when you weren't. He was kind, he... he helped me when no one else would."

WG's gaze dropped to her belly, his face contorted with rage. "And now you carry his child," he said bitterly. "While I was out there, fighting to make a life for us, you were here, betraying me."

"It wasn't meant to be like this," Hannah pleaded. "I didn't want to hurt you."

WG's mind spun, the weight of Hannah's betrayal hitting him harder than any punch he'd taken in the ring. His thoughts blurred as anger, sorrow, and disbelief clashed within him. He shook his head, trying to keep his voice steady, though the pain in his chest was undeniable. "Well, you have," he said, his tone cold and distant. "And now, I've no choice but to leave again."

Hannah's eyes filled with desperation, her voice trembling. "Leave? Where will you go?"

WG's gaze hardened. The answer was clear in his mind, the only place that had ever truly felt like sanctuary. "Liverpool," he replied, the words clipped. "To Janie's. I need time to think... to figure out what to do next."

He turned from her, feeling the sting of her betrayal echo in every step. His heart, heavy with confusion and hurt, sought solace in the only place that had ever given him peace—the familiar streets of Liverpool. There, he could sort through the wreckage of what his life had become, away from the chaos and pain that now filled his home.

"Please, Will," Hannah begged, reaching out to him, but he stepped back, avoiding her touch.

"It's too late for that, Hannah," he said, his voice flat and final. "You've made your choice, and now I'll make mine. I'm going to Liverpool, and when I return, we'll see what becomes of this mess."

Without another word, WG turned on his heel and walked out, leaving Hannah sobbing in the cold, empty room. The door closed behind him with a heavy thud, sealing the fate of their fractured relationship. As WG left the workhouse, his heart hardened by betrayal; he knew there was no turning back. He would go to Liverpool to his half-sister Janie. He needed time to think and to plan his next steps. Confronting Tom now would solve nothing. He needed to gather his thoughts, figure out what to do next, and reflect on the life that had unravelled so quickly.

WG stepped into Janie's warm kitchen, his heart heavy from the events of the past few days. The familiar scent of tea filled the air, offering a small comfort as he sat across from his elder half-sister. Janie's eyes were filled with concern, reflecting the deep bond they shared, built through years of family struggles and triumphs.

After what felt like hours of silence, WG finally spoke, his voice strained with the weight of his confession. "It's all come undone, Janie. Hannah… she's pregnant, and it's not mine." The words landed like a punch, his fists clenched as if to hold back the tidal wave of frustration. "I don't know what to do."

Janie reached across the table, resting her hand gently on his. "You've been through hell, WG. But running won't fix what's broken. Stay here, with me. We'll figure this out—together."

WG nodded slowly, as though testing the thought. "I can't go back to that life. I need a fresh start… here, in Liverpool. Maybe this is where I'm supposed to be."

A soft smile spread across Janie's face, her eyes bright with hope. "This has always been home, hasn't it? You'll find your way. We'll make sure of it."

In that moment, for the first time in days, WG felt a glimmer of something new—a flicker of possibility. Liverpool, with Janie by his side, could be the place where he finally healed, where he could rebuild not just his life, but a sense of purpose.

They continued to talk, sifting through the fractured pieces of his life in Coventry, and eventually, the conversation shifted. "There's someone I want you to meet," Janie said thoughtfully. "Her name's Catherine. She works down by the docks—strong, smart. I think you two might get along."

WG looked at her curiously, unsure if he was ready for such a step. The pain from Hannah's betrayal was still raw. "Catherine? What makes you think she'd want anything to do with me?"

Janie's smile widened knowingly. "She's been through her own battles, WG. She's tough, but she's kind. And I think she could help you see there's still a future—one better than the past you've left behind."

WG was quiet for a moment, letting the idea sink in. Liverpool had always felt like home, and maybe Janie was right. Maybe this was where his new beginning could take root. He gave her a small nod, a smile creeping onto his face. "Alright. Introduce us. Let's see what happens."

Janie squeezed his hand, her voice filled with optimism. "It's time for you to heal, WG. And maybe Catherine will be part of that journey."

Later that week, WG met Catherine. She was just as strong and resilient as Janie had described, with a sharp wit and a quiet strength that drew him in. As they spent more time together, WG began to picture a life not marked by past mistakes but by the promise of something better. Catherine had her own scars, and in each other, they found a shared understanding of loss and the will to move forward.

With Janie's support and Catherine's companionship, WG could finally see a future where the pain of the past no longer defined him. Liverpool, once a sanctuary, now offered the hope of rebuilding—a new life, perhaps even one with Catherine by his side.

Liverpool's familiar sights and sounds welcomed WG to those who frequented the alleys and docks. The city that had shaped his youth now beckoned with a mixture of nostalgia and regret, its streets winding like a labyrinth of memories. WG walked with purpose, his mind filled with resolve and the weight of recent revelations.

One afternoon amidst the bustling marketplace near Lime Street Station, WG's eyes scanned the crowds and, with astonishment, identified the figure of Tom Green—the man who had turned his world upside down. The city's cacophony masked the turmoil within WG, a tempest of emotions stirred by betrayal and shattered trust.

There, amidst the swirl of vendors and passersby, WG caught sight of Tom, whose broad frame and uncertain demeanour betrayed his recognition of the man approaching him.

"Tom Green," WG's voice rang out, cutting through the noise like a blade. "I didn't expect to find you here."

Tom turned slowly, his features tightening with a mixture of guilt and defiance. "WG," he replied, his voice subdued yet tinged with apprehension. "What brings you back to Liverpool?"

WG's jaw clenched as he fought to contain the torrent of emotions threatening to spill forth. "You know why," he said evenly, his gaze piercing. "You took advantage of my trust. You dishonoured our friendship."

Tom swallowed hard, his gaze flickering as he struggled to find the words. "WG, I never meant for—"

"For what?" WG interrupted sharply. "For Hannah? For my family?"

The marketplace seemed to hold its breath as WG and Tom stood face to face, the weight of years of friendship and now betrayal hanging heavy between them.

"You betrayed me," WG continued, his voice resonating with pain. "You took what was mine."

Tom's expression softened, a flicker of regret crossing his features. "I'm sorry, WG," he said quietly. "I never wanted to hurt you."

WG shook his head slowly, his voice tinged with bitterness. "But you did," he replied, the words heavy with accusation. "You hurt us all."

Silence settled over them, broken only by the distant cries of street vendors and the distant hum of city life. WG's fists clenched at his sides, his heart heavy with the weight of betrayal and loss. His gaze bore into Tom's, searching for any hint of remorse or sincerity. Slowly, he nodded, a gesture laden with resignation. "You've made your choice, Tom," he said quietly. "Now you'll live with it. She is with your child".

Tom's heart pounded in his chest as the full weight of WG's words sank in. The marketplace noise faded into the background, leaving only the charged silence between the two men. Tom could feel the blood draining from his face, his mind reeling with the realisation that WG knew everything—and more.

"I didn't plan it," Tom replied, his voice trembling as he tried to explain the unexplainable. "You were gone, WG, and she was alone. We didn't mean for it to happen. It just... it just did."

WG stepped closer, his face a mask of controlled anger. "Don't you dare try to justify it? You knew she was my wife. You knew, and still, you crossed that line. And now, because of it, there's a child—your child."

Tom felt a wave of nausea wash over him as the reality of his actions came crashing down. He had betrayed his wife, his family, and the man who had been like a brother to him. The weight of his guilt was suffocating, and he struggled to find the words to make it right, though he knew there was no way to undo the damage.

"I'm sorry, WG," Tom finally managed, his voice barely above a whisper. "I never wanted this to happen. I never wanted to hurt you or Jane or Hannah. I was weak, and now... now everything's ruined."

WG's eyes blazed with anger, but there was a deep, simmering pain beneath it. "Sorry isn't going to change what's done," he said coldly. "You've destroyed everything, Tom. Not just for me but for Hannah and Jane, too. What do you think happens to her now? To that child?"

Tom hung his head, the full extent of his betrayal crushing him. "I'll take responsibility," he said, though the words felt hollow. "I'll do right by Hannah and the child. I'll—".

"You'll what?" WG cut him off, his voice laced with bitterness. "Leave your wife and children to raise this child? Destroy your own family to try and fix the one you helped break? It's too late for that, Tom."

Tom had no answer. The reality of his situation had trapped him in a nightmare of his own making, with no clear way out. He felt the sting of WG's words as if they were physical blows, each one driving home the truth of his actions.

WG stepped back, his expression hardening. "I'm leaving," he said, his tone final. "I don't want to see you, Tom. Not ever again. You've made your bed, and now you'll have to lie in it."

With that, WG turned and walked away, leaving Tom standing alone in the crowded marketplace, his world crumbling around him. The man who had once been his closest friend was now lost to him, along with everything else he had taken for granted. Tom watched WG disappear into the throng of people, feeling more alone than he had ever felt in his life.

With those words, WG turned away, his steps echoing against the cobbled streets as he walked away from Tom Green and the echoes of their shattered friendship.

As he navigated the familiar alleys of Liverpool, WG felt the weight of his fractured marriage and turbulent past pressing upon him. The city that offered promise and opportunity momentarily held only shadows and regrets, its bustling streets a stark reminder of the choices that had led him here.

Yet amidst the turmoil, WG found a flicker of determination—a resolve to rebuild, to reclaim his sense of honour and purpose, and to forge a new path forward, away from the echoes of betrayal and loss.

With its towering docks and bustling streets, Liverpool bore witness to the turbulent chapters of WG's life—a life shaped by hardship, resilience, and the quest for redemption. As he walked through the city's labyrinthine alleys, WG carried with him the echoes of his fractured marriage and the wounds that refused to heal, each step a testament to the complexities of love, loyalty, and the relentless pursuit of a brighter tomorrow.

By the early 1880s, Tom Green's world in Liverpool had unravelled like the frayed threads of a once-proud tapestry, worn thin by the relentless passage of time and the weight of his own mistakes. The Byron family, whose respect he once valued, now viewed him with disdain that cut deeper than any wound. The revelation of his infidelity with Hannah—WG's wife—had struck like a thunderclap, shaking the very foundations of the households involved. Jane's father, once a steadfast ally and source of financial support, turned his back on Tom, his disappointment evident in every word and gesture.

"You've shamed us all, Tom," Mr. Byron had declared, his scowl etching itself permanently into his features. "Jane deserved better than you, running off to Coventry and bringing disgrace upon this family."

The words had stung, but Jane's icy reception pierced Tom's heart. Her eyes, once filled with love and trust, now bore the look of a woman betrayed. The home they had built together, filled with the laughter of their children, now echoed with an uncomfortable silence, a void left by the shattered trust.

The scandal spread like wildfire through the streets of Liverpool, where secrets were whispered behind every closed door. Tom found himself cast out from the society he once took pride in being a part of. He sought solace in the dimly lit taverns of Warrington, where old friends offered hollow words of comfort but no reprieve from the guilt gnawing at his soul.

Meanwhile, tension brewed between Tom and his brother, Dickie, in Birmingham. The bond that once tied them together as brothers was now strained under the weight of Tom's actions. Dickie, who had married Jane's sister Elizabeth, found himself caught in the crossfire of family loyalties. The scandal poisoned their relationship, turning once joyful gatherings into tense and uncomfortable affairs.

"You've made a real mess of things, Tom," Dickie had said during one of their strained exchanges. "Do you not see the pain you've caused Elizabeth, Jane, and the whole family?"

Tom had no answer, only a heavy sigh as he looked away. The weight of his guilt pulled him down like a stone in his chest. The family he had once been so proud to be part of now felt like an anchor, dragging him further into despair.

In this state of desolation, Tom found his way back to Coventry, not triumphant—but as a man humbled by the consequences of his own actions. The return to Hannah and their child, Harry, was not the joyful reunion one might have hoped for. Instead, it was a reluctant acceptance of responsibility, a life of penance for the mistakes that had led him down this path.

Coventry, a city that once promised new beginnings, now held only the stark reality of his chosen life. The financial hardship that followed was relentless. No longer supported by Jane's father, who had severed all ties after the scandal, Tom was left to fend for himself. The loan that once seemed like a lifeline now became a burden, the repayments a constant reminder of the support he had squandered.

WG, weary from his own turbulent journey, stepped in as a reluctant peacemaker. His own life had been marred by the same storm that had torn Tom apart, and perhaps in that shared misery, he found a sliver of empathy. But there was more to his intervention—he wanted to ensure that his children with Hannah had a better upbringing, free from the chaos that had defined their lives thus far.

"Tom," WG had said during one of their rare and sombre meetings, "you need to mend what's left. Jane... she's hurting, but there's still the children if you've got the strength to face it."

But, burdened by his guilt and the spectre of his failures, Tom could only nod in weary acknowledgement. The road ahead was uncertain, fraught with the consequences of his past actions and the challenge of rebuilding a life from the wreckage he had caused. The financial strain, the disapproval of those he once called family, and the fractured relationships that now defined his existence were all the bitter fruits of his choices. And as he stood on the threshold of a new chapter, one thing was painfully clear—there was no going back, only the arduous task of moving forward, one faltering step at a time.

For Hannah, the following years were marked by a crucible of resilience, hardship, and a tumultuous relationship with Tom. Their love was undeniable, but it was a love as fierce and unpredictable as the stormy skies that often loomed over their lives. Their intense and consuming connection was marred by bitter arguments that sometimes erupted into violent clashes. The unpredictability of their bond left both scarred, physically and emotionally, setting them on a downward spiral that always seemed to hover dangerously close to the abyss of the workhouse for Hannah and her children.

On many nights, their voices would echo through the narrow streets of Coventry, their quarrels spilling out from behind closed doors.

"You never think, Tom!" Hannah would cry, her voice choked with frustration. "You've no regard for what you put us through—no thought for the children, for me!"

His face flushed with anger and guilt, Tom would lash out, "And what about you, Hannah? Always naggin', always findin' fault. Ain't I done enough, haven't I tried? What more do you want from me?"

Their fights would rage until exhaustion overtook them, only for reconciliation to follow in the quiet of the night. Tom would take her hand, his voice softened by regret. "I'm sorry, Hannah. I don't mean to hurt you, you know that. It's this cursed life, this endless struggle. But I love you, I do. I can't bear to see you suffer."

Hannah, tears glistening in her eyes, would nod, her heart torn between love and despair. "And I love you, Tom. But we can't go on like this. We need to find a way for the sake of the children."

In 1886, when Hannah discovered she was with child again, the news came as both a shock and a glimmer of hope. "Tom, I'm with child," she whispered one evening, her voice trembling with a mixture of fear and anticipation.

Tom, who had been staring into the fire, turned to her, his face a mask of conflicting emotions. "Another one?" he muttered, more to himself than to her. Then, after a pause, he reached out to place his hand on her swelling belly. "We'll make it work, Hannah. We have to."

Their second child, Joe, was born later that year. His arrival brought a brief respite to their troubled lives, a fragile thread of happiness that both clung to in the midst of their turmoil. But the peace was short-lived. As the years passed, so did the strains on their relationship. Tom's temper, once a fleeting shadow, now emerged with a ferocity that left scars on both their hearts.

By 1893, their lives had spiralled further into darkness. The shadow of their shared past loomed large, and the tensions between them reached a breaking point. The streets of Coventry whispered of their violent arguments, of the nights when Hannah would flee with the children to the safety of a neighbour's home, only to return when Tom's rage had subsided.

One fateful day in June of 1893, Tom's anger boiled over into a public spectacle. The courtroom buzzed with hushed whispers as the charges against him were read aloud—assault and threats, his temper finally leading him to the brink of disaster.

Hannah stood as the complainant in the dimly lit courtroom, her face pale but resolute. She had seen too much and endured too much to let fear guide her now. Dishevelled and hollow-eyed, Tom stood in the dock, the weight of his actions pressing down on him like a heavy shroud.

"You're in custody for another offence," the magistrate intoned, his voice stern and unyielding. "And now you're summoned for threatening Hannah Griffiths of Hill Street. What do you have to say for yourself?"

Tom's voice was barely above a whisper. "I never meant to harm her, Your Honour. It's just... sometimes, the world gets too much."

The magistrate's gaze was cold. "The world gets too much for many, Mr. Green, but that's no excuse for violence."

As the sentence was passed, Tom's shoulders sagged with the weight of his punishment. He was to be sent to jail, his freedom stripped away as a consequence of his actions.

For Hannah, there was no victory in this. The man she had loved, the father of her children, was lost to her in more ways than one. She returned to the small almshouse on Hill Street, where she now resided with her children—Harry and Joe. It was a place of refuge but also a stark reminder of how far they had fallen. The workhouse loomed ever closer, its shadow a constant companion to the frailty of their existence.

When the children were asleep in the quiet moments, and the streets outside were silent, Hannah would sit by the window and gaze out into the darkness. She had survived, but at what cost? The man she had once loved was now a ghost in her life; his presence was felt only in the echoes of their past.

But even in the depths of despair, she had a flicker of resilience. She had her children, and she would endure for them. The storm that had torn through her life had not broken her, and as long as she had breath, she would continue to fight—not just for survival but for a future where her children might know a life free from the shadows that had haunted hers.

John Plant

In the spring of 1877, during the balmy days when the sun cast its golden rays upon the dusty roads of England, William Griffiths—known in the prizefighting circuits as "Shiny"—first encountered young John Plant. The meeting was fortuitous, born from an incident that only the most capricious of fates could have orchestrated. Shiny, then touring the countryside with a band of prizefighters, each more hungry for glory than the last, had stopped in a small, unassuming village to partake in the local festivities.

The village, a quaint patch of earth nestled between rolling hills and fertile fields, was alive with the sounds of merriment. The air was thick with the scent of roasted meats and the laughter of children chasing one another in carefree abandon. Among the crowd of onlookers and revellers, Shiny's discerning eye caught sight of a lad no older than eighteen, his build lean yet sinewy, his eyes ablaze with the spirit of youth and the fire of ambition.

As he was introduced to Shiny by the village farrier, John Plant had the look of a lad who had seen hardship, yet it had not worn him down; rather, it had tempered him like steel in a forge. There was a rawness to him, an unpolished potential that, to Shiny's seasoned gaze, was akin to discovering a rough diamond amidst common stones.

"Aye, you've got the makings of a fine fighter," Shiny remarked after observing John deftly sparring with an older youth. The crowd, though small, was rapt with attention as

John's fists flew with surprising speed and accuracy, each strike a testament to his budding talent. "But you've much to learn if you're to make your mark in the ring."

John, still catching his breath, looked up at Shiny with a mix of admiration and defiance. "I can hold my own," he replied, wiping the sweat from his brow. "But I'd welcome the chance to learn from the likes of you."

Thus began the unlikely apprenticeship between the seasoned veteran and the eager novice. Seeing in John the spark of something greater, Shiny took him under his wing. Their journey together was one of grit and determination, with Shiny imparting the wisdom of years spent in the ring. He taught John the art of strategy, the importance of stamina, and the value of knowing when to strike and when to hold back. They travelled from town to town, with Shiny acting as John's second, a steadfast presence in his corner during bouts that grew increasingly challenging.

Under Shiny's tutelage, John Plant blossomed into a prizefighter of renown; his name whispered in the alleyways and shouted from the rooftops. The crowds grew larger, the stakes higher, and with each victory, John's reputation swelled until he was considered a force to be reckoned with—a man who could draw a crowd simply by the mention of his name.

Shiny had always known the circus wouldn't last forever. After years of dazzling crowds, the constant travel and grueling routines began to wear on him. The battles with his grief had waned and he longed for a quiet simplicity of home.

A place he hadn't seen in far too long. One crisp morning, he made the decision to retire from the ring. It wasn't easy leaving behind the whirlwind of lights, laughter, and applause, but he knew it was time.

Though he hung up his gloves and left the ring, Shiny never lost touch with John. The two had grown close during their time together, John always fascinated by Shiny's discipline and agility. Now, John's career as a prizefighter was taking off, his natural strength and determination catapulting him to fame. Shiny kept in contact, cheering John on as he continued to rise in the prizefighting ranks. They exchanged letters, John's full of tales from the ring, victories hard-won, and challenges faced. Shiny offered advice where he could, though their paths had diverged. Their bond, born in the chaos of the circus, remained strong even as their lives took them in different directions.

It was only a short time before the promoters of more prestigious bouts sought after the lad who had once sparred for sport in a village square. The pinnacle of his career seemed within reach, and with it came the inevitable letter—one that carried with it both respect and a humble request. John Plant, ever loyal to the man who had shaped him, wrote to Shiny with a proposition that appealed to friendship more than to business.

"Dear Will," the letter began, written in the unsteady hand of a man more accustomed to fists than penmanship. "There's a grand fight on the horizon, in Coventry no less, that could make or break my standing in this game. I ask of you, not as my tutor, but as my friend—will you stand as my second once more?"

John mentioned that the purse for the fight was handsome indeed—a sum that would line the pockets of both fighter and second, win or lose. But more than the money, which was considerable even by Shiny's standards, there was the promise of the thrill, the tension of the crowd, and the intoxicating scent of victory in the air. And, of course, there was the prospect of the bookmakers' gold, ever a temptation for a man of Shiny's inclinations.

Shiny, although retired from the ring as a fighter, would not resist the call. The thrill of the sport still pulsed through his veins, and the chance to see John Plant—his protégé— reach the heights of success would be an opportunity he could not pass by.

By the time John Plant's letter reached WG, he had already left behind the rough-and-tumble life of prizefighting in his mind. But decision to be John's second had to be made and would not come easily. Prizefighting had been a large part of his life, but the years had taken their toll. His once nimble feet were now slower, his reflexes dulled by countless blows to the head, and the thrill of the fight no longer burned as brightly as it once had.

Liverpool became his refuge—a bustling port city where he could disappear into the crowd, leaving behind the reputation that had followed him through every small town and village across England. The transition was difficult. For a man who had lived by his fists, the quiet routine of civilian life was alien. But Liverpool, with its teeming docks and labyrinth of narrow streets, offered him a chance to start anew, far from the blood-stained rings where he had made his name.

Shiny found work as a railway worker in Liverpool, and his strength was still an asset even if it was no longer used to falling opponents. The labour was hard, the hours long, but it was honest work. He could come home each night with his head held high, his earnings modest but sufficient to keep a roof over his head and food on the table. The rough camaraderie of the docks reminded him of the fight circuit but without the ever-present threat of violence. Here, he was simply William Griffiths, another face in the crowd, and that was just how he wanted it.

Despite the physicality of his work, WG often found his mind drifting back to the days of his youth, to the roar of the crowd, and the rush of adrenaline before a bout. He missed the strategy, the mental chess of a fight, even as his body reminded him why he had walked away. The old injuries ached in the damp Liverpool air, his knuckles swollen from years of punishment, and his vision blurred slightly in one eye from a particularly brutal match. These were the reminders of the price he had paid for his time in the ring.

His past, though left behind, was not entirely forgotten. Occasionally, a fellow dockworker would recognise him, a glint of recognition in their eye as they recalled his fighting days. These moments were rare, and WG preferred to keep them that way, brushing off any enquiries with a gruff word or a change of subject. He had little interest in reliving those days—his focus now was on maintaining the simple, steady life he had carved out for himself in Liverpool.

But the letter from John Plant changed everything. The young man's words brought with them memories of the time Shiny had taken him under his wing, of the potential he had seen in the boy, and the pride he had felt watching John grow into a formidable fighter. Their bond was strong, forged in the heat of battle and the trials of the road. And now, after a few years apart, John was reaching out to him, not as a mentor but as a friend, asking for his guidance in what could be the most important fight of his career.

WG read the letter several times, each word stirring a mix of emotions within him. There was certainly pride in what John had become, but also a deep sense of foreboding. He knew the dangers that came with the sport, the toll it took on a man's body and soul. And yet, despite his reservations, WG felt the old pull of the ring, the undeniable urge to be part of the world he had once been part of.

The letter from John painted vivid scenes of the prizefighting world, and with each description, WG felt something long dormant stir within him. The fire that had once driven him, the spirit that had earned him the name Shiny, wasn't gone—it had only been waiting. The thrill, the challenge, the life of the ring—it all called to him, louder with each passing day.

And though WG had hung up his gloves, he realised now that Shiny, the fighter within, was never far away. Slowly, the idea began to form that maybe, just maybe, it was time for Shiny to make a return. Not as a fighter under the big top, but as someone who could guide John, stand by his side, and once again immerse himself in the world he knew so well. Shiny would rise once more—not for the applause, but for the fight.

After a long night of contemplation, WG finally made up his mind. He retrieved a worn pen from a drawer and began to write his reply, the decision weighing heavily on him.

"My Dear John," he wrote, the words flowing slowly, deliberately. "I shall be honoured to stand by your side in Coventry. Let us win this one together."

As he sealed the letter and prepared it for the post, Shiny came alive and he knew that his quiet life in Liverpool was about to be briefly disrupted. The call of the ring was one he could not ignore, not when it came from John. He would return to that world if only for a short while, to help the young man who had once looked up to him with such admiration. But this time, he told himself, it would be different. He would go to Coventry and see John through this fight.

And so it was that Shiny was to make his way to Coventry, not as the man he once was, but as the seasoned second to a fighter whose future shone bright with promise. The streets of Coventry, familiar yet ever-changing, would welcome him back with a warmth that belied the tension in the air. The fight ahead would be no ordinary bout—it was a chance for redemption, for glory, and for one last dance with the ghost of his former self. And of course, there was Hannah and the children there too.

The summer of 1881 had laid a heavy hand upon the streets of Coventry, its sweltering heat interspersed with the distant hum of the city's restless pulse. WG found himself drawn back to the city. In the heart of this changing town, it was not the allure of familial ties that beckoned him but rather the siren call of prizefighting and the temptations that accompanied it. Once celebrated in the ring, his name had been shadowed by a few years of inconspicuousness on the road and in Liverpool. But the scent of opportunity, the promise of easy money, and the thrill of the gamble were enough to lure Shiny back to Coventry.

It was an afternoon like many others when Shiny stepped off the train, the familiar sights and sounds washing over him like a long-forgotten melody. His heart, a fighter's at the core, thrummed with excitement and apprehension. The familiar cobbled streets, the brick façades of pubs, and the endless chatter of Coventry's denizens seemed to whisper of old glories and untamed ambitions.

His first stop was the local tavern, where the air was thick with smoke and the atmosphere charged with stories of past matches. Shiny, clad in a well-worn suit that had seen better days, entered with the ease of a man accustomed to both admiration and suspicion. The patrons, recognising him immediately, greeted him with a mixture of awe and trepidation.

"Aye, if it isn't Shiny himself!" exclaimed an old acquaintance, Tom Rawlings, a broad-shouldered man with a face marred by years of scrapping. "What brings you back to Coventry? I thought the bustle of Liverpool had you in its grip."

Shiny, accepting a pint of ale from the bartender, settled himself at a corner table. "Tom," he said, his voice carrying the gravelly undertones of a man who had seen both triumph and ruin. "It's good to see familiar faces. I've come back for a bit of business and perhaps to see how the old town fares."

Tom raised an eyebrow. "Business, eh? Word has it there's a prize fight planned for next week. A proper bout with stakes high enough to draw the attention of even the most hardened of gamblers."

Shiny's eyes lit up with a gleam that betrayed his interest. "Is that so? Tell me more about this fight."

As Tom began to recount the details—of rival fighters and clandestine meetings—Shiny's mind raced with possibilities. The lure of the money, combined with the thrill of betting and the potential for a high-stakes fight, grew. His past glory in the ring was about to clash with his present self, and the temptation of a quick gain was too potent to resist.

Shiny's next days were a flurry of activity. He reacquainted himself with old allies and rivals while laying the groundwork as second in the upcoming fight. The excitement and tension that accompanied his preparation reminded him of the old days when each bout was a step closer to fame—or infamy.

But amidst the fervor of prizefighting, Shiny also sought personal closure. He reached out to Hannah, the woman he had once called his own, now burdened with the weight of their troubled past. The meeting was set in a quiet corner of the town's market, a place that once resonated with their shared history.

Hannah, her face etched with the lines of hardship and weariness, looked up as Will approached. Though tired, her eyes held a glimmer of the defiant spirit that had once drawn him to her.

"Will," she said softly, her voice carrying a blend of relief and apprehension. "You've returned?"

Will nodded, his gaze softening as he took in her worn appearance. "Hannah. I've come back not just for the fight that is the gossip of the town but to see you and the children."

Hannah's expression was a mix of acceptance and sadness. "The children need you, Will. But I fear the life you lead will only bring more trouble."

Will sighed, the weight of his choices pressing down upon him. "I've made my share of mistakes, Hannah. But I wish to find a way to set things right—for their sake and mine."

The conversation was difficult, filled with unspoken regrets and hopes for redemption. As they talked, the subject shifted to Richard, their youngest son now on the cusp of eight or nine years old. Will's thoughts drifted, considering the boy's future.

"Hannah," he said cautiously, "how are things with you and Tom? How is Richard?"

Hannah's face fell, the weariness deepening in her features. "It's been hard, Will. Tom tries, but we struggle to keep food on the table. The work is scarce, and Richard often goes to bed hungry. He doesn't understand why things are this way, and it breaks my heart."

Will felt a pang of guilt at her words. "But surely, it can't be that bad?"

Hannah looked away, her voice thick with emotion. "You don't see the desperation, Will. I try to keep a brave face for Richard, but the truth is, I can't sustain this life for him much longer. I'm terrified of what he's growing up in. He needs stability—something we can't provide."

Will clenched his fists, a surge of compassion overwhelming him. "And Tom? How is he handling it?"

"Tom is a good man, but even he feels the weight of it all," she admitted, her eyes glistening with unshed tears. "He loves Richard, but he can't fill the gap that your absence has left. Richard often asks about you, and I dread having to explain why his father isn't here. It's tearing me apart."

The gravity of her words hung heavily in the air, and Will contemplated the reality of their situation. "I never wanted it to be like this, Hannah. I want to be there for him."

A silence enveloped them, thick with unspoken emotions. Will's heart raced as he considered the implications of her plight. "What if I took Richard with me to Liverpool?" he proposed suddenly, the thought forming in his mind. "He could have a home with Catherine and me. He wouldn't have to struggle like this anymore."

Hannah's eyes widened, a mix of disbelief and fear. "You want to take him away? Just like that? He's my son, Will!"

"I know," he said urgently, "but you just said it yourself. You can't keep going like this. Richard deserves a chance—a life where he doesn't have to worry about his next meal or where he'll sleep at night. I can provide that for him."

Hannah's voice trembled as she replied, "And what of me? You'd just cut me off from him? I don't want to lose him, Will."

Will stepped closer, a deep resolve in his eyes. "It wouldn't be about cutting you off. We can find a way to make it work, to show him he's loved by both of us. But he needs stability. You need stability."

Hannah took a shaky breath, the weight of her circumstances crashing down on her. "If you truly believe this is best for him… I just hope he knows he is loved, no matter where he ends up."

With that, the past hung heavily between them, but the possibility of a new beginning for Richard glimmered faintly on the horizon.

The Golden Cross Inn, a relic of the old Coventry Mint with its timbered beams and flickering lanterns, was the meeting place for men whose lives were entwined with the raw sport of prizefighting. In the dim light of a corner booth, Shiny found himself seated across from John Plant, the young fighter whose future was as uncertain as it was promising.

"Shiny," Plant began, his voice thick with the weight of the upcoming bout, "I need your guidance, your hand in my corner. This fight… it's more than just another bout. It's everything."

WG nodded slowly, his eyes narrowing as he considered the young man before him. "Aye, lad, I see it in your eyes. The hunger, the drive. But it's not just fists that win a fight—it's wits. And the ring. It's no place for mercy."

Plant leaned forward, his hands trembling slightly. "I've no use for mercy, not in the ring. But I need you there, Shiny. You've seen more of this world than I ever will. I need your wisdom, your calm when the crowd roars and the blows start flying."

WG took a deep breath, his gaze steady and unyielding. "You'll have it, lad. I'll be there. But understand this—once you step into that ring, it's you against the world. I can guide you, but you'll need to find the strength within yourself to finish the fight."

Plant nodded, determination hardening his features. "I'll not let you down, Shiny. Together, we'll make sure this fight is remembered."

The two men clasped hands, the pact sealed with a firm grip and a shared look of understanding. As they left the Golden Cross Inn, the weight of the forthcoming bout hung heavy in the air, a silent testament to the trials ahead.

The sun set on Coventry as Shiny prepared for the days ahead, the weight of the past lightened by the prospect of what was to come.

The day of the fight arrived with the kind of oppressive heat that made the air feel thick and heavy. The ring was set in a secluded spot on Hearsall Common, a location chosen for its privacy. Spectators gathered in hushed anticipation, their eyes fixed on the fighters who would soon step into the centre.

Now fully immersed in the role of a second to John Plant, Shiny was a figure of intensity and focus. He moved through the crowd with practised ease, his presence a testament to his former prowess in the ring. But as the fight began, the brutality of the contest and the sheer violence on display were stark reminders of the price that came with such spectacles.

The ring, a rough-hewn square of dirt and sawdust encircled by a raucous crowd, had become a stage for a grim spectacle. The evening air was thick with anticipation and the acrid smell of sweat, tobacco, and cheap ale. Lanterns flickered in the dusk, casting long, eerie shadows on the faces of the gathered crowd, their eyes gleaming with a blend of excitement and dread. The stakes were heavy with the weight of pride, reputation, and the fierce will of two men who had staked all on this brutal contest.

Samuel Arnold stood opposite John Plant, a hulking figure whose presence alone seemed to dim the lights. Like granite mallets, his fists had already left their mark on many an opponent, and tonight, he was determined that John would be no exception. The crowd's murmurs of support for the young Plant were muted, their cheers tentative, as if they sensed the cruelty of the bout that was to unfold.

John Plant, leaner but not lacking in resolve, met Arnold's cold gaze with a determined glare of his own. His body bore the scars of countless hours of training, every muscle honed, but as the first blows were exchanged, it became clear that this fight would test him beyond anything he had faced before. The first round passed with a flurry of fists, each man probing the other, feeling out weaknesses, but as the fight dragged on, it devolved into a test of endurance and sheer will.

"Keep your guard up, lad," Shiny's voice, hoarse from years of barking commands, rang out from the corner, cutting through the din of the spectators. "He's strong, but he ain't faster than you. Outlast him, and the fight's yours!"

John nodded, sweat and blood mingling on his brow, his breath coming in laboured gasps. The pain was immense, every muscle screaming for relief, but he pressed on, fuelled by the voice of his mentor and the fire that still burned in his heart. But Arnold was relentless. With each round, his blows grew heavier, his attacks more savage, driving John to the edge of his endurance.

The turning point came in the ninth round. Seeing his chance, Arnold delivered a brutal uppercut that caught John square on the chin. The world around him seemed to spin; the lantern light turned to streaks of gold as his vision blurred. The crowd's roar became a distant, muffled echo. He staggered, legs wobbling beneath him, and for a moment, it seemed as though he might fall.

"Stand firm, John!" Shiny's cry cut through the haze, a lifeline to which John clung desperately. "Don't let 'im see you falter, lad! Show 'im what you're made of!"

John's knees buckled, but he somehow remained on his feet, driven by sheer force of will. But Arnold, sensing victory, pressed his advantage. Another punishing blow to the ribs left John gasping for breath, and then a fierce hook to the temple sent him crashing to the ground. The crowd erupted into a frenzied roar as John lay in the dirt, unmoving, save for the ragged rise and fall of his chest.

"John!" Shiny's voice was now tinged with desperation as he rushed to his side. The old fighter knelt by his pupil, his heart pounding not from the exertion of his own past battles but from the fear that he had pushed the young man too far. John's face was pale, his eyes fluttering as he struggled to stay conscious. "You've done more than enough, lad. It's over. There's no shame in yielding now."

But John did not respond. His breath had slowed to a terrifying stillness. His body battered beyond recognition, refused to stir. Shiny's heart sank as he saw the blood pooling beneath John's head, dark and ominous against the dirt.

"Get a doctor!" Shiny's voice, usually so commanding, was now thick with panic as he looked around wildly, but the crowd, sensing something far worse than a mere defeat, began to draw back in horrified silence. Once a spectacle, the fight had turned into a tragedy before their eyes.

Shiny cradled John's head, his hands trembling. "John, stay with me, lad," he whispered, his voice cracking with emotion. But the young fighter's eyes, once so full of fire, now stared blankly at the darkening sky.

The doctor arrived, his face grim as he examined the fallen fighter. He looked up at Shiny, his expression confirming the worst. "He's gravely injured. We must get him home immediately."

The aftermath of the fight descended into a maelstrom of confusion and despair. As the crowd dispersed, their earlier excitement replaced by a sombre hush, John Plant was carried from the ring, his body limp and unresponsive. The air, once filled with the roars of the onlookers, now seemed thick with dread, as if the night itself mourned the terrible turn of events.

As they rushed him to Tom Rawlings' lodgings with all haste, John's condition worsened with each passing yard. The dimly lit streets of Coventry seemed endless, each cobblestone jolting his battered frame, his breaths coming in shallow, ragged gasps. By the time they reached his modest lodgings, the flicker of life within him was waning. Physicians were summoned, their faces grave as they worked with desperate urgency, but the damage was too severe. The once indomitable spirit that had driven him through countless battles was now fading, slipping through their fingers like sand.

Through the long hours of the night, as those who loved him watched in helpless anguish, John Plant's strength ebbed away. Despite the best efforts of those around him, he succumbed to his injuries, the fight having claimed more than just his body—it had stolen his future, his dreams, and the hope that had burned so brightly in his heart.

As the dawn broke, the room was filled with a heavy silence, the weight of loss pressing down on all who remained. Grief settled like a shroud over those who had known him, and as word spread of his untimely death, the city was gripped by a profound sense of outrage. What had begun as a contest of strength and skill had ended in tragedy, leaving behind a fallen fighter and a wound in the hearts of all who had cheered for him, believed in him, and seen in him the promise of something greater.

The police, having received word of the fight, were quick to act. Shiny and several others found himself caught up in the ensuing investigation. The subsequent days were a blur of police interrogations, courtroom proceedings, and a relentless press. Shiny's name, once associated with heroism and glory, was now mired in controversy.

John Plant's death struck WG with a force more brutal than any blow he had ever taken in the ring. The young man who had once looked up to him with eyes full of hope and determination was gone, his life snuffed out in the very sport that had once given WG purpose. As he sat alone in the candle-lit cell, the weight of his grief bore down upon him, a crushing sorrow that left him hollow and bereft.

WG stared at his reflection in the cracked mirror, seeing not the hardened prizefighter he had once been but a man who had lost his way. The death of John Plant was a stark reminder of the life he had chosen—a life that, for all its fleeting glories, had led to ruin and despair. The realisation that he had played a part in the young man's downfall was more than he could bear.

Tears welled in WG's eyes, unbidden and unstoppable. He buried his face in his hands, the sobs shaking his frame as he mourned not only for John but for the countless others who had fallen victim to the same harsh world. It was in this moment of overwhelming grief that WG made a vow—he would turn his back on this life of violence and vice forever.

With a heavy heart, WG knew that his days as "Shiny" were over. The thrill of the fight, the allure of the wager, the roar of the crowd—none of it mattered anymore. All he saw were the faces of those he had lost, the lives destroyed by the very thing he had once loved. If able, he resolved to leave Coventry, to leave the world of prizefighting behind, and to seek redemption in a life far removed from the shadows of his past.

The trial was a spectacle in itself. The Coventry Herald detailed the events with a grim determination, capturing the essence of the case and the characters involved. The courtroom was filled with tension as Shiny and the other accused were brought before the magistrates.

WG, despite his past fame, found himself facing serious charges. Yet, in a stroke of fortune or perhaps due to the lack of concrete evidence linking him directly to Plant's death, he was acquitted. The verdict brought a mixture of relief and lingering unease, leaving WG to contemplate his future.

As WG prepared to leave Coventry, his thoughts were consumed by the well-being of his children, particularly the youngest, Richard. The turbulence that had defined their lives, compounded by Hannah's ongoing struggles, weighed heavily on his heart. WG knew that Richard needed stability, something that seemed increasingly elusive in their current circumstances. Determined to offer his son a better chance at a steady life, WG resolved to take Richard back to Liverpool with him. He believed that a fresh start in the familiar surroundings of Liverpool, where family ties were stronger and the support was more certain, would provide Richard with the foundation he needed to thrive.

Richard was a source of both hope and trepidation. WG's decision to take him was a testament to his desire to provide stability and a chance for a better life.

His journey back to Liverpool was solemn, filled with reflections on the choices he had made and the path that lay ahead. As he reunited with Catherine and his new family, the weight of his past lingered, but he was determined to forge a new path. The prospect of a fresh start in Liverpool, away from the shadows of prizefighting, offered a glimmer of hope.

Catherine greeted WG with a mixture of relief and cautious optimism. "You've returned," she said, her voice carrying the warmth of a homecoming. "And with Richard in tow."

WG nodded, his expression weary but resolute. "Yes, Catherine. It's time to put the past behind me and focus on building a future for ourselves and the children."

The days followed were filled with efforts to integrate Richard into their new life and establish a semblance of normalcy. WG found solace in the work available in Liverpool—even returning to the watchmaking trade. Though known, his reputation as a prizefighter was a shadow that he hoped would gradually fade.

The presence of Richard, now a young boy with dreams and aspirations of his own, was both a challenge and a source of motivation. WG's desire to shield him from the stigma of his past was a driving force, influencing his decisions and actions.

As the months passed, WG and Catherine navigated the complexities of their new life, working to provide stability and security for their family. Though never entirely erased, Shiny's past became a part of the broader tapestry of their lives—a reminder of the choices made and the path to redemption.

The shadow of prizefighting continued to linger, occasionally surfacing in whispers and glances. Yet, WG was determined to build a future where his past was no longer a defining force. There were many challenges, but the promise of a fresh start in Liverpool was a beacon of hope, guiding him towards a new beginning.

Growing up amidst the changes, Richard came to understand the significance of his father's past and the efforts made to distance themselves from it.

As WG looked out over the streets of Liverpool, he felt a renewed sense of purpose. The journey from Coventry had been fraught with trials, but it had also provided an opportunity.

1898

The year 1898 had dawned upon Coventry with a bitter chill, casting long shadows over the ancient city's cobbled streets and bustling markets. Queen Victoria's reign, now in its twilight, had painted the globe in the imperial hue of British pink—a testament to the far-reaching dominion of the British Empire. Yet, amidst the grandeur of empire and the march of progress, the streets of Coventry bore witness to a different kind of struggle—a battle not waged with rifles and bayonets but with the silent scars of domestic strife and unspoken fears.

Coventry, a city with a rich history of weaving and watchmaking, had seen its traditional industries slowly wither under the relentless tide of change. The looms that once hummed with the production of fine silk and ribbons now stood silent, their wooden frames gathering dust as the demand for hand-woven goods waned in the face of mechanised production. The city's famous watchmakers, whose intricate timepieces had once been the pride of England, found themselves displaced by cheaper imports and the relentless march of factory-made goods. The once-bustling workshops, where artisans had laboured with meticulous care, now echoed with the silence of obsolescence.

But as one chapter closed, another was being written in Coventry's storied history. The resilient city began to reinvent itself in the face of industrial decline. Once a modest venture, the bicycle industry had burgeoned into a booming enterprise. The streets, once filled with horse-drawn carriages and pedestrians, now thrummed with the steady rhythm of bicycle wheels. Coventry had become the beating heart of Britain's bicycle industry, with factories springing up to meet the insatiable demand for this new mode of transport. Names like Rudge-Whitworth, Ariel and Singer had become synonymous with innovation and quality, and their bicycles were sought after not only in Britain but across the globe.

The success of the bicycle industry laid the groundwork for an even greater transformation. As the century began to draw to a close, it sees the birth of a new industry—motor vehicles. Pioneers like James Starley and Harry Lawson had sown the seeds. John Kemp Starley had recently renamed his company The Rover Cycle Company (that would later make motorbikes and cars under that name). By 1898, the first motorised vehicles began to sputter and roar through Coventry's streets. The city's factories, once dedicated to bicycles, began to adapt to the production of motorbikes and, eventually, the nascent automobile. The names of Daimler and Humber became synonymous with this new era of transportation, their factories humming with the sound of progress.

Yet, amidst this industrial rebirth, the remnants of Coventry's past lingered like ghosts. The once-proud weavers, now displaced by mechanisation, struggled to find their place in this new world. The watchmakers, their craft no longer in demand, faced an uncertain future. The city, caught between the old and the new, was a place of contrasts—where the gleaming promise of the future stood alongside the faded glory of the past.

For the people of Coventry, these changes brought both hope and hardship. The booming bicycle and motor industries offered new opportunities but also demanded sacrifices. The long hours in the factories, the relentless pace of production, and the constant pressure to innovate took their toll on the workers. The city's skyline, once dominated by church spires and medieval towers, now bristled with the chimneys of factories, their smoke mingling with the mist that rolled in from the surrounding countryside.

Against this backdrop of industrial transformation, the personal struggles of its inhabitants played out in quiet corners and crowded tenements. The growth of new industries did little to ease the poverty that still gripped many of Coventry's residents. Families like those of Hannah and Tom Green navigated their own battles, the relentless march of progress doing little to alleviate the daily hardships they faced.

In the midst of this burgeoning modernity, the old world still casts its long shadows. The city, with its rich tapestry of history, stood at a crossroads—a place where the past and future collided, creating a landscape as complex and varied as the lives of those who called it home.

Hannah's life with Tom was fraught with turbulence, marked by periods of uncertainty and violence. While there were moments when things seemed calm, these were often overshadowed by Tom's increasingly volatile behavior. His temper flared unpredictably, and as his frustrations grew, so did his cruelty. Tom's violent outbursts often left Hannah not only physically bruised but also emotionally shattered. The hope that things might improve was slowly eroded with each incident, leaving her in a state of constant fear.

Eventually, the situation grew so dire that Hannah was forced to seek refuge in the Almshouses on Hill Street with the childern, a grim marker of how far she had fallen from the life she had once imagined. These Almshouses, intended for the destitute, provided comfort, and they were a sanctuary of sorts from the violence at home. However, they could not shelter her from the overwhelming sense of despair that accompanied her. The children, Harry and Joe, were no better off. At times, the family had been placed in the Workhouse, where many poor families ended up during these desperate times, as a harsh place—barely more than a shelter for the destitute, with grim conditions that mirrored the family's impoverishment. The children endured long, punishing days of labour, their youthful spirits dimmed by the weight of their surroundings. The family had reached rock bottom, with little in the way of hope or escape. Harry and Joe, too young to fully comprehend the breadth of their circumstances, were forced to grow up quickly in the face of such adversity.

Destitution marked every aspect of Hannah's life during this period. She struggled not only to survive but also to maintain some sense of dignity amidst the squalor. Her existence had become a brutal cycle of survival, with violence from Tom haunting her past and the unforgiving walls of the Almshouses and Workhouse defining her present.

In the dim light of a grey February morning, the narrow alleyways of Pepper Lane stood cold and unforgiving, much like the man who now approached his partner with dark intent. Tom Green, once a man of dreams, now a figure worn down by bitterness and selfishness, stood before Hannah, his eyes gleaming with a desperation that chilled her to the core.

"Hannah," Tom began, his voice low and rough, "where are the newspapers? I need them."

Hannah, determined to make ends meet in any way she could, took to the streets as a newspaper vendor. Every morning, she would collect a bundle of freshly printed papers, taking them in lieu of sale from the local printer. With a sharp eye and a practised shout, she would position herself at the busiest corners, where the foot traffic was thick, and the noise of the city was a constant hum. She hawked the papers at face value, her voice cutting through the din as she called out the day's headlines, hoping to catch the attention of passersby.

As the hours wore on, Hannah's energy never flagged. Each sale meant a little more money for her and her children—Harry and Joe. A few more coins to stretch toward their meagre subsistence. At the end of the day, she would return to the printer with the unsold papers, her hands rough and ink-stained from the long day's work. After deducting the costs, the small residue she kept was a hard-earned reward, a testament to her resilience and determination to provide for her family.

Hannah's heart pounded as she met his gaze, understanding all too well the consequences of his demands. "I won't give them to you, Tom," she replied, her voice firm despite the fear rising within her. "You know what'll happen if I do. I'll be in debt to the newspaper owner, and there'll be no way out for me or the children."

Tom's expression hardened, his temper flaring. "Debt?" he scoffed, stepping closer, his tone menacing. "That's your worry? I need those papers, and I'm not askin' for your permission."

Hannah's hands clenched at her sides, her resolve unshaken. "You don't need them, Tom. You're not thinkin' of me or the children. You're only thinkin' of yourself, as usual." She paused, her voice trembling with anger and sadness. "You've never once provided for us, never cared how we manage to get by. And now you want to drag us even deeper into the gutter?"

Her words struck a nerve, igniting Tom's rage. "Don't you talk to me like that, woman!" he snarled, his hand shooting out to grab her arm. "You think you can deny me? After all, I've done?"

"Done?" Hannah shot back, wrenching her arm free. "What have you done but bring us misery? I'm the one who's kept a roof over our heads, the one who's scraped and saved to feed our boys. And now you want to take the little we have left?"

The fury in Tom's eyes flared like wildfire, and in that instant, all reason fled. He lunged at her, his fists flying in a blind rage, determined to take what he believed was his by right.

"Think of the children, Tom!" Hannah cried, trying desperately to shield herself from his blows. "Think of Harry and Joe! They need me!"

But Tom was beyond reason, his mind consumed by the anger that had simmered for so long. The narrow street bore witness to the violence, the sounds of the struggle echoing down the street.

"Stop it, Tom!" a voice suddenly shouted, alarmed by the noise, rushed in. "You'll kill her, you monster!"

Several bystanders, drawn by the commotion, followed, their faces pale with horror as they pulled Tom away from the crumpled form of his wife. Hannah lay on the cold floor, her face battered and bruised, her right side limp and unresponsive. Blood trickled from her nose and mouth, her eyes wide with shock and pain.

"Get the constable!" someone shouted, and within moments, a police officer arrived, his stern gaze falling upon the scene of domestic ruin. Tom, his breath coming in ragged gasps, was dragged away in handcuffs, his once-defiant expression now hollow and vacant.

Hannah was lifted gently by the women who had gathered, her body trembling as they laid her on the cobbled street. She tried to speak, but the words would not come. Her right side remained motionless, the terrible realisation of paralysis setting in as she stared blankly.

"Poor soul," one of the women murmured, her eyes filling with tears. "She's been through so much, and now this…"

As the day passed, the bruises on Hannah's face and eyes deepened, her condition worsening as the extent of her injuries became clear. A neighbour described her as paralysed on her right side, and her once lively voice was now reduced to a pained whisper. She was barely able to move, the life slowly draining from her broken body.

Hannah's decline was agonisingly slow. Her breath became shallow, each exhale a fight, as if her body clung to life even as it slipped through her fingers. She rarely spoke, and when she did, it was in barely audible fragments of what once had been her vibrant voice. There was no relief from the constant ache, no respite from the creeping numbness that took over her right side, leaving her trapped within her own failing body. The effort to lift even a hand or turn her head had become too great. The home, once filled with her energy and bustling activity, was now reduced to hushed whispers and the soft shuffling of feet, as those who loved her waited helplessly for the inevitable.

Despite the efforts of those who cared for her, Hannah's strength waned. Her eyes, once bright with life, grew distant, as if she had already begun her slow journey to another place, far from the suffering that held her captive. Every passing moment felt like an echo of loss, as she slipped further away from the world she once knew.

The room was quiet, the air heavy with the sorrow of knowing that Hannah Parker's time was slipping away. Her children stood around her bed, their faces etched with grief and helplessness. She lay motionless, her body frail and bruised, the evidence of Tom Green's brutal attack still visible on her skin. The right side of her body was paralysed from the vicious beating, her once-strong figure now fragile and broken. Her breath came in shallow gasps, and though her eyes fluttered open from time to time, she was barely aware of her surroundings, drifting in and out of consciousness.

Tom Green, the man who had once been her husband, the father of Harry and Joe, was in prison, awaiting trial for what he had done to her. The thought of him hung like a dark cloud over the room, but no one spoke his name. There was too much pain, too much anger, for words.

Harry Green stood at the foot of the bed, his fists clenched so tightly his knuckles were white. He had always tried to be strong for his mother, to protect her from his fathers outbursts. But in the end, he had been powerless to stop the violence that had left her like this. Now, he was forced to watch her suffer, helpless in the face of the damage Tom had inflicted. His voice, usually so confident, was now barely a whisper. "Mum... I'm here. I'm right here." His words hung in the air, unanswered, as her half-open eyes fluttered weakly, unfocused.

Joe Green, only 12, sat beside the bed, clutching his mother's limp hand, tears streaming down his face. He hadn't understood, not fully, until now. The fear that had gnawed at him for years—every time Tom raised his voice or lashed out—had finally come to pass, and it was worse than he could have imagined. "Mum," he whispered, his voice trembling with desperation. "Please wake up. Please. We need you."

Hannah's eyes opened for a brief moment, a flicker of recognition in her gaze. Her lips moved slightly, as if she was trying to say something, but no sound came. The paralysis had stolen her voice, and the sight of her struggle to speak broke Joe's heart. He let out a sob and gripped her hand tighter, as though holding on would somehow keep her with him.

Lizzy Cribdon, her eldest at 35, was seated on the other side of the bed, her face pale and drawn with grief. She had taken charge since the attack, caring for the boys and managing what was left of their broken family. "Mum, you don't have to fight anymore," Lizzy whispered softly, brushing a strand of hair from Hannah's face. "We'll be alright. You've done enough. We'll take care of the boys now. You can rest."

Beside her, Bill Griffiths stood quietly, his arm around her shoulder. He had seen violence before—seen its ugly consequences—but nothing had prepared him for watching the family unravel like this. His eyes were dark with sorrow, but he remained a steady presence, knowing there was little he could do but be there for them.

Martha Preston, Hannah's youngest daughter, stood near the window, her back turned as she stared out into the cold, dreary evening. Her hands shook, and she wiped at her eyes, trying to keep herself together. The image of her mother lying there, broken and helpless, was too much to bear. "Mum," she whispered to herself, almost too quietly for anyone to hear, "this isn't how it was supposed to be."

A faint rustle drew their attention back to the bed as Hannah's chest rose and fell, each breath more laboured than the last. Her eyes opened once more, a faint spark of awareness in them. She looked at her children—Harry, Joe, Lizzy, Martha and Bill—and for a brief, fleeting moment, they saw the mother they knew. But it passed just as quickly, her gaze unfocused again, the effort too much for her broken body to sustain.

Harry swallowed hard, his voice thick with emotion. "I'm going to take care of Joe, Mum. Don't you worry. I won't let anything happen to him. I swear it."

Joe, still holding her hand, sobbed uncontrollably, his voice barely audible through the tears. "Please don't leave us, Mum. Please."

Lizzy leaned in closer, her own tears falling softly onto the bedsheets. "We love you, Mum. We always will."

There was no response, just the slow, fading rhythm of Hannah's breathing. The bruises on her skin seemed even more stark in the candlelight, a painful reminder of the violence that had stolen her life piece by piece. The paralysis had left her unable to speak, unable to move, but her presence—her love—still filled the room, even as it slipped further from their grasp.

In her final moments, Hannah's breathing slowed, her chest barely rising. The children watched in silence, knowing the end was near, though none of them wanted to accept it. And then, with a final, quiet exhale, she was gone.

The silence that followed was suffocating. Joe buried his face in the bedsheets, his sobs muffled but heart-wrenching. Harry stood frozen, his tears finally spilling over as he stared at the still figure of his mother. Lizzy pressed her hand to her mouth, trying to stifle her own sobs, while Bill moved closer, his arm tightening around her.

Martha turned from the window, her face wet with tears, and walked over to her mother's side. She placed a gentle hand on Hannah's forehead, her voice trembling. "She's at peace now," she whispered, more to herself than to anyone else. "No more pain."

Though Hannah's life had ended in violence and suffering, in that room, surrounded by her children, her love endured. They had survived Tom's cruelty, and now, in her memory, they would have to find a way to survive without her. Together.

The post-mortem revealed the truth—the extensive effusion under the scalp at the seat of the bruising, the engorged blood vessels, and the fatal rupture within her brain. The cause of death was apparent, even if justice was not.

At the inquest, the medical officer, Dr. Samuel Turner, took the stand and laid out the grim details while Tom Green sat in silence, his face a mask of regret and denial. His testimony delivered in the measured, clinical tone expected of his profession. He adjusted his spectacles and began to outline the grim details of Hannah Parker's condition.

"The deceased, Hannah Parker, exhibited extensive bruising and contusions, particularly on the right side of her body. There were signs of severe trauma to her head and chest, consistent with repeated blows. The right side of her body was paralysed, likely a result of injury to the brain, which I believe may have been caused by the force of an assault. The bruises were deep and extensive, suggesting significant force was used."

The coroner nodded, urging him to continue, as the room sat in silence.

"While it is clear that the injuries sustained in the beating played a significant role in Mrs. Parker's deterioration," Dr. Turner continued, "I must state, however, that she was in a weakened condition prior to the assault. Although the blows undeniably contributed to her demise, I cannot categorically state that they were the sole cause of death. There were underlying factors—her weakened constitution and lack of proper circulation—that may also have contributed to her passing."

The coroner leaned forward, his brow furrowing. "So, Dr. Turner, are you suggesting that while the injuries were severe, they were not the definitive cause of death?"

Dr. Turner hesitated briefly, choosing his words carefully. "I am suggesting, sir, that the injuries were a major factor, but not necessarily the only factor. Her death was the result of a combination of the injuries and her subsequent inability to recover due to her already fragile condition."

Tom Green sat still, his eyes cast downward, but the weight of the medical officer's words hung heavily in the room, leaving little doubt in anyone's mind as to the true cause of Hannah's untimely death.

The coroner, his voice stern and unyielding, addressed Tom with words that cut deeper than any blade.

"I can only say you are a very fortunate man indeed," the coroner declared, his eyes fixed on Tom. "You have been helped all around by good fortune, and the evidence has not been strong enough for me to convict you of manslaughter. But know this, Thomas Green—although the legal part of it is not complete, it is in the minds of the jury, and in my mind too, that you have in some way contributed to Hannah's death. If I speak for an hour in censure, I could not add one word more than this: we consider you morally responsible for the death of the person you have been living with."

Tom's head hung low as the coroner's words echoed through the room, the weight of his guilt pressing down on him like a millstone. Though he had escaped the gallows, the burden of his actions would haunt him for the rest of his days, a spectre of the life he had destroyed.

As the coroner dismissed the court, the people of Coventry whispered amongst themselves, their faces marked with sorrow and indignation. They had witnessed the fall of a woman who had lived through hell and endured more than any soul should bear. As they left the courtroom, the chill of that bitter February morning seemed to cling to them, a reminder of the cold, hard truths that had been laid bare—truths that would forever shadow the life of Thomas Green.

Later that fateful year, the streets of Coventry bore witness to another chapter in Thomas Green's troubled existence—a man whose once-vibrant life had descended into disarray, tainted by the twin spectres of drunkenness and disorder. As winter's cold, unforgiving winds swept through the city, Thomas stood once more before Alderman Maycock and Mr F. W. Franklin, his gaunt figure betraying the toll of a life unravelling at the seams.

The courtroom was a sombre theatre of justice, its wooden benches worn smooth by the countless cases heard within its walls. The murmur of spectators filled the air; their curiosity tinged with the stark anticipation of another failed redemption. Police constable Carpenter took the stand, his evidence a stark indictment of Thomas's descent. With a steady voice, he recounted the events of that fateful night.

"I found the defendant," Constable Carpenter began, "in a state of extreme inebriation upon Smithford Street. His behaviour was most disorderly. He was shouting and flailing about, causing a considerable disturbance."

His face drawn and pallid, Thomas rose from his seat, his eyes blazing with a desperate defiance. "I protest this, sir!" he declared, his voice trembling with indignation. "I am not the man they make me out to be. It was but a slight indulgence—nothing more!"

His brow furrowed with the weight of the evidence before him; Alderman Maycock leaned forward. "Mr. Green, this marks your twelfth appearance before us. The court has grown weary of such excuses. The pattern of your behaviour leaves little room for doubt."

Tom's voice rose, cracking under the strain. "It is not fair! It is not just! What of those who drive others to despair? What of those who conspire against me? I am a victim of circumstances, nothing more!"

Mr. F. W. Franklin, his spectacles gleaming in the dim light, peered at Thomas with a mixture of pity and resolve. "The law must be applied with impartiality, Mr. Green. Your record speaks for itself. The sentence, as it stands, is a fine of five shillings and costs."

The words fell like a final verdict upon Thomas. His shoulders slumped, the fire of defiance dimming into resignation. "I have no means to pay," he muttered, the weight of his fate pressing heavily upon him. "If only there were justice in the world…"

With the sentence pronounced, Thomas was escorted out of the courtroom, his footsteps echoing hollowly against the stone floor. The meagre fine, a sum he could not hope to gather, ensured his return to the confines of a prison cell—a stark reminder of his unending cycle of regret and redemption.

As the echoes of Thomas Green's footsteps faded into the silence of his prison cell, Coventry carried on—a city straddling the precipice of progress and the weight of its own history. The cobbled streets, glistening with the frost of a new year, whispered tales of resilience and redemption, their stones bearing witness to the ebb and flow of human endeavour amidst the relentless march of time.

Hannah Parker's memory lingered like a spectral presence in the quiet corners of Pepper Lane, where shadows danced upon worn cobblestones. Her tragic end, a silent testament to a life cut short by violence and circumstance, wove through the lives of those who had known her. The dim light that filtered through the cracks in the narrow street seemed to carry her spirit—a poignant reminder of the fragile threads that bind us all and the enduring struggle for justice in a world that often seemed indifferent to its own cruelties.

Richard Griffiths

The chill of spring had descended upon Coventry, casting a sombre veil over the city's cobbled streets and ancient architecture. The leaves, once vibrant in their autumnal splendour, now lay scattered across the ground, their colours fading to a dull brown. Richard Griffiths stood at the edge of the cemetery, the brisk wind carrying the chill of early February through his coat. As the final shovelfuls of earth were laid upon his mother's pine casket, he felt a profound sense of finality settle over him.

The mourners had long since dispersed, their hushed conversations and rustling of skirts replaced by an eerie silence. The clouds overhead mirrored the heaviness in Richard's heart—a blanket of grey that seemed to absorb the warmth of the world. His mother, Hannah, had been laid to rest, and with her passing, Richard felt the weight of his family's future pressing heavily upon his shoulders.

As he stood alone by the graveside, Richard's thoughts wandered back through the tumultuous years that had led him to this point. He remembered his early childhood in Coventry, a time marked by hardship and instability. His father, WG, had been a fleeting presence in his life—a travelling prizefighter whose bouts were overshadowed by his frequent disappearances. WG's erratic behaviour and broken promises often shattered the promise of a stable family life.

Richard's earliest memories were of the Coventry Poor Law Union Workhouse, where he had spent his early years. The workhouse, a grim institution of discipline and deprivation, was a place of constant struggle. It had housed Richard, his mother, younger siblings, and his grandfather, Will Parker. Despite the harsh conditions, the workhouse was also a place where Richard had learned resilience and resourcefulness. He recalled the stern faces of the workhouse matrons, the clatter of wooden spoons on tin plates, and the solemn prayers recited before each meagre meal.

In 1881, WG returned to Coventry for a brief period, bringing with him the promise of a more stable future for Richard. But the promises were short-lived. The turmoil of Tom Green and Hannah Parker and WG's own instability created an environment fraught with uncertainty. Richard, then only nine or ten years old, was whisked away from Coventry's familiar yet turbulent streets to the bustling city of Liverpool. It was a bittersweet departure—leaving behind the only home he had known yet escaping the constant chaos that marked his early life.

Liverpool, with its busy docks and vibrant streets, was both a refuge and a new source of anxiety. Now living with his partner Catherine and her young son John, WG presented a new family dynamic that Richard had to navigate. The city was a world away from the sombre workhouse and the drab streets of Coventry. Richard found himself thrust into a household where he was expected to find a place amidst new faces and unfamiliar routines.

Despite the fresh start, Liverpool brought its own set of challenges. Richard tried to adapt to his new surroundings, but the scars of his past remained. He took young John under his wing, mirroring the care he had once shown to his half-brother Harry in Coventry. The city was a mixture of promise and struggle, its opportunities shadowed by the weight of Richard's unresolved past.

Richard's life took another turn when his father, Catherine, and their young son, John, embarked on a journey to Yorkshire, lured by the prospect of a better life as watchmakers. Left behind with Auntie Janie and her family, Richard felt a fresh wave of loneliness surge within him, mingling with a complex blend of relief and sorrow. The stability of Auntie Jane's home offered a comforting sanctuary, yet the departure of another parent left an ache that was difficult to ignore. Despite the familiar rhythm of Liverpool and Auntie Janie's nurturing presence, Richard grappled with the weight of his unresolved past. The city's promise seemed tinged with melancholy, every street and alley a reminder of the family he had lost. Nevertheless, Richard steeled himself, determined to forge a new path amidst the echoes of his former life, clinging to the hope of building something enduring from the fragments of his troubled history.

Richard's teenage years were marked by the continued struggle to reconcile his past with his present. Although Auntie Janie provided a nurturing home, Richard's heart remained burdened by the ghosts of Coventry and the abandonment he felt when his father moved away. With its sprawling docks and bustling streets, Liverpool offered opportunities and challenges. He worked diligently to support himself, taking on various jobs that kept him busy but never quite fulfilled. His formative years were spent grappling with the echoes of a fractured family and the harsh realities of urban life. Amidst the backdrop of Liverpool's vibrant yet gritty landscape, Richard sought solace in the rhythms of daily work and the rare moments of respite offered by Auntie Janie's home. Within this setting, he began to shape his future, yearning for something more stable and fulfilling to anchor him.

Richard's life took a significant turn in this new city when he met Alice Royle. Alice, a spirited young woman from a stable and supportive family, offered Richard a stark contrast to his tumultuous upbringing. Their connection was immediate and deep, and despite their informal status, their commitment to each other grew stronger over time. Their bond was a beacon of hope, offering Richard a sense of belonging and stability that had been elusive throughout his childhood.

However, These years in Liverpool were marked by joy and sorrow. Richard and Alice's burgeoning family was hit hard by the loss of Alice's father in 1892 and the untimely death of their infant sons, John and William, over the next four years. The grief was a heavy burden, but the support they found in each other's company made the weight bearable. Their relationship grew deeper as they navigated through their shared sorrow, finding solace and strength in one another.

In the midst of their trials, a beacon of hope arrived with the birth of their third child, Richard, in 1897. The arrival of this new baby brought a profound sense of joy and renewal to their lives. The little boy's cries filled their home with a vibrant, life-affirming energy that had been sorely missed; for Richard and Alice, the birth of their son was not just a moment of personal happiness but a symbol of their resilience and their ability to rebuild amidst adversity. The sight of their healthy baby sleeping peacefully in his cradle was a balm for their weary hearts, offering a glimpse of a brighter future and a new beginning for their family.

In early 1898, however, Richard received the news of his mother's death, prompting his return to Coventry for the funeral. The journey back was tinged with the anticipation of facing a past from which he had long tried to distance himself.

Standing beside the freshly turned earth, Richard was joined by his siblings. Lizzy, now married and settled, greeted him with a mixture of relief and sadness. Martha, who had married Bill Preston, and the young boys Harry—whom he had known as a boy—and Joe, half-brothers now all but orphaned with their father in prison and their mother dead.

Richard's heart ached for Joe, who was close to the age he'd been taken to Liverpool. He now faced a future fraught with uncertainty as he did at the same age. As he approached Joe, the boy's wide-eyed gaze met his own. "What will become of you, young man?" Richard asked softly, his voice laden with concern.

Joe looked up at him, his face a canvas of confusion and fear. "I don't know, Richard," he replied quietly.

Richard's resolve hardened. He had been a protector since his own childhood, and now, he would extend that protection to Joe. "You'll come with me," he said firmly. "Alice and I will take care of you. You'll have a home with us in Liverpool."

The decision was made amidst the grief and chaos of the funeral. Richard and Alice would provide a stable environment for Joe, offering him the family and security he so desperately needed. Though money was tight, and the challenges ahead were daunting, Richard was determined to break the cycle of hardship that had plagued their family for generations.

WG's unexpected arrival in Coventry was a shock to the family, stirring a whirlwind of emotions in the wake of Hannah's death. After years of almost estrangement, he had made his way back from Yorkshire, driven by a newfound urgency to reconnect with his children and ensure their well-being amidst their grief. His presence was as surprising as it was poignant, arriving unannounced at Lizzy's home on Stoney Stanton Road.

The day WG arrived was overcast, the clouds casting a muted light over the cobbled streets of Coventry. Lizzy, who had spent the past days mourning her mother and tending to her own family, opened the door to find her father standing on the threshold. His weathered face, marked by the passage of time and his hardships, bore the burden of years spent away from his children. Though heavy with regret, his eyes were also filled with a determined resolve.

"Elizabeth," WG said softly, his voice betraying a hint of weariness. "I hope I am not intruding."

Lizzy studied her father for a moment, her emotions a tumultuous blend of surprise and scepticism. The sight of him stirred up a complex mix of memories and feelings. "Father," she replied, her tone cautious but not unkind. "It's been a long time. What brings you here?"

WG stepped into the modest home, removing his hat and revealing a mane of greying hair. "I've come to see how you all are faring," he said. "After your mother's passing, I felt it was time to come back and be of some support if you'll have me or need me."

The reunion was marked by a silence that spoke volumes. Lizzy's wariness was palpable, her eyes searching WG's for signs of sincerity. Despite the decades of distance and the unresolved issues between them, she could not deny the sense of relief at seeing her father.

"Very well," Lizzy said, her voice steadying. "Come in. We have much to discuss."

As WG entered the modest parlour, the atmosphere was charged with a quiet, unspoken tension. The room, decorated with simple furnishings and the soft hues of mourning, seemed to hold its breath as the family confronted the reality of their altered dynamic. WG's arrival was a poignant reminder of the gaps left by Hannah's absence, and as he settled into a chair, he looked around at the family he had left behind.

Lizzy's husband, with a glance of acknowledgement, offered WG a seat while Lizzy busied herself while preparing tea. "We've had our share of sorrow," Lizzy began, her voice betraying a hint of strain. "But we're managing as best we can."

WG nodded, his expression reflecting both regret and resolve. "I wish I could have been here sooner," he said. "I've been remiss in not being more present. But now, I am here to make amends and to support you all in any way I can."

The conversation that followed was a mixture of cautious exchanges and guarded confessions. Lizzy spoke of their difficulties, while WG offered what he could—not only in words but in his presence. The weight of their shared history loomed large, yet the meeting held the promise of a renewed connection, however fraught it might be.

As the family gathered to share their experiences and reconcile with the past, WG's return marked the beginning of a new chapter in their lives. His presence was a testament to the complexities of family and the enduring ties that bind them, even in the face of adversity.

The decision had been made with careful deliberation: Lizzy would take responsibility for Harry, while Joe would move to

Liverpool to live with Richard. It was a decision born from the desire to offer some semblance of stability and familial care for the children left in the wake of Hannah's death and Tom Green's troubled existence. Lizzy and Richard's resolve to provide homes for their late mother's children, despite the complexities and past grievances, spoke volumes about their character and the enduring bonds of family.

WG, now seated in the parlour of Lizzy's home, gazed around at the gathered family with a mixture of satisfaction and paternal pride. The gravity of the decisions made weighed on him, yet he found solace in the commitment shown by his children. His eyes softened as he observed the decisions of Lizzy and Richard and their resolve to protect and nurture their half-siblings amidst their own trials, reflecting their innate goodness. The sight of Lizzy's tender care for Harry and Richard's willingness to open his home to Joe was a testament to the compassion that still thrived despite the years of separation and past misunderstandings.

Elizabeth approached her father, her demeanour one of quiet determination. "Father," she began, her voice steady, "I believe it's for the best that Harry stays here with us. He'll have the stability of a familiar environment and the support of family."

WG nodded appreciatively. "Your decision is a wise one, Elizabeth. It warms my heart to see the love and care you and Richard are providing for the children."

With the practicalities settled, WG's thoughts turned to the next steps. He was keen to ensure that all loose ends were tied up and that Richard, in particular, understood the full scope of their plans and intentions. During their family discussions, WG proposed a meeting with Richard to formalise their arrangements and address any outstanding matters.

"Richard," WG announced, his voice carrying the authority of a man who had long been away but now sought to make amends. "I suggest we meet tomorrow at the Golden Cross Inn. It's a fitting place for us to discuss the future and ensure we are all on the same page."

The Golden Cross Inn, with its warm, inviting atmosphere and reputation as a neutral ground for such meetings, was chosen for its familiarity and historical significance in their lives. It was a place where old wounds could be addressed and new understandings forged over a hearty meal and a pint of ale.

Elizabeth nodded in agreement, understanding the importance of this meeting. "Very well, Father. I'll make sure Richard is informed of the time and place."

As WG looked around at his Lizzy's family, his heart swelled with a mixture of pride and hope. The path ahead was fraught with challenges, yet the unity and determination displayed by Lizzy and Richard gave him confidence that they would navigate the complexities with grace. The decision to reunite and support one another, despite the past, was a testament to the enduring power of family bonds.

The following day, as WG prepared for the meeting at the Golden Cross Inn, he reflected on the unexpected turns his life had taken. The prospect of reconciling with Richard and solidifying plans for Harry and Joe was a significant step forward. With a sense of purpose and a heart filled with hope, WG set out to bridge the gaps left by years of separation and to build a future grounded in understanding and mutual respect.

The Golden Cross Inn had been the setting for the uneasy reunion between father and son. WG's voice was rough, and he felt regret as he spoke. "I never intended for things to turn out this way," he said, his gaze heavy with unspoken apologies. "I should have done more for all of you."

Richard had looked at his father with a mixture of empathy and resolve. "What's done is done, Father," he said quietly. "What matters now is Joe and Harry's future."

WG's visit had also included plans for Joe to meet his Uncle Dick in Birmingham the following day. The journey to Birmingham was a hopeful gesture, a chance to connect with the remnants of their extended family and offer Joe a glimpse into his heritage. Richard agreed.

When Richard, WG, and Joe arrived at Dick's home, the atmosphere was charged with anticipation. Dick, surprised by WG's appearance, greeted them with a mixture of astonishment and wary warmth. "WG," Dick said, his eyes widening, "this is a sight I never expected. After all these years…"

WG nodded, his face marked by years of regret. "Dick. It's been too long. Now give these boys a seat and a cup of tea." as he strode over his old friends threshold.

Inside, Dick's wife, Elizabeth, welcomed them with a calming presence, though her emotions were a complex mix of delight and apprehension. She had long awaited this moment, and seeing WG after so many years was a mixture of joy and wariness. Elizabeth's face softened with genuine pleasure, though her eyes sparkled with the memory of WG's mischievous escapades. The memory of his cheeky, wicked ways lingered like a shadow over her smile.

Tea was served, and the room's atmosphere lightened as Dick and WG reminisced about their youth. The clink of china and the warmth of the fire seemed to ease the tension that had lingered since WG's arrival. The conversation shifted, becoming more personal and less laden with the gravity of recent events.

Dick, leaning back in his chair, his eyes reflecting the dancing flames of the hearth, addressed Joe with a twinkle of curiosity. "And what do you wish to become, Joseph?" he asked, his voice gentle and probing yet infused with genuine interest.

Joe, with his small hands clasped around his cup of tea, responded earnestly, "I want to learn, Uncle Dick. Perhaps even become a butcher, like my grandfather—as WG has told me."

Dick's eyebrows lifted in surprise, his face brightening with a smile. "A butcher, you say? Your grandfather was a respected one, you know. A fine craftsman of the trade." His voice was laced with pride, and he glanced at Elizabeth, who nodded in agreement.

"Aye, indeed," Dick continued, his tone nostalgic. "He was well-regarded in his day. His shop was the finest in Liverpool. People would come from far and wide to buy his meat. His skills were unmatched, and his integrity was second to none. You know, people spoke of him with great respect. It was said that he had a knack for selecting the best cuts and a talent for butchery that made his shop the talk of the town."

Elizabeth added, "Your grandfather had quite the reputation, Joe. His name was synonymous with quality, and the respect he earned was well-deserved."

The room's atmosphere lightened further, with the shared laughter and understanding bridging the gap between past and present. The notion of Joe following in his grandfather's footsteps was embraced warmly, and the respect for the family's heritage seemed to knit the room together in a shared sense of pride.

As the conversation turned more personal, WG regaled them with tales of his own youth, the stories punctuated by laughter. "Ah, the old days," WG said, his eyes twinkling with a mixture of mischief and fondness. "Those were the times, weren't they? What scrapes—Dick and I, quite the pair of rascals back then." Dick chuckled, nodding in agreement. "Indeed."

WG's laughter rang out, rich and full, his eyes gleaming with the memory. "Ah, and how could I forget the time Tom coaxed me into the boxing ring on Hillock Street?" He shook his head, chuckling at the mischief of it all.

The stories of their youthful escapades painted a vivid picture of a time when the world seemed full of endless possibilities and adventure. The camaraderie and the mischief of their younger years were a testament to their enduring bond despite the passage of time and the changes in their lives.

The conversation soon turned to more recent matters, and Dick's gaze grew serious. "Now, regarding Joe's future," he said, "I'll write to the family in Liverpool to ensure he has the opportunity to work as a butcher's apprentice when he is old enough. It's a chance to honour the legacy of your grandfather and to give Joe a path forward. It's only right that he be given the chance to learn the trade and continue the family's esteemed tradition."

Joe's eyes widened with excitement, his hopes for the future taking shape with the encouragement and support of his extended family. "Thank you, Uncle Dick," he said, his voice filled with gratitude and anticipation. "I'll do my best to make you all proud."

Richard spoke of his hopes for the future despite the weight of past tragedies and the discussion touched upon Tom Green, Joe's estranged father, whose absence loomed large over their family. Richard's muted references to Tom's failures and misfortune highlighted the distance that had grown between them. "Tom's troubles have been many," Richard said quietly, "but we must focus on the future for Joe's sake."

Joe's curiosity about his half-siblings in Liverpool was met with gentle explanations. "They are your half-brothers and sisters," Dick said, his tone soothing. "They live not far from where you'll be settling, and I'm sure they'll be glad to meet you in good time. It's important to keep the family ties strong despite the many changes we've all faced."

The conversation wound down as the evening grew darker, but the sense of unity and understanding lingered. WG and Dick made plans to follow through on their commitments, ensuring that Joe's future would be one of opportunity and hope. The warmth of the hearth and the promise of a new beginning provided comfort as they faced the challenges ahead, bound by the legacy of their past and the hope for a brighter future.

1901

The summer of 1901 brought a languid warmth to the streets of Liverpool as the sun cast long shadows and stirred memories in a city caught between its storied past and its emerging future. Richard Walters, once known as Richard Griffiths, stood on a familiar street corner overlooking the bustling Mersey. The river mirrored the relentless passage of time and the changes it had wrought in his life with its ceaseless flow and the constant hum of activity along its banks. The decision to change his name was not one he had taken lightly; it was a deeply personal act of reinvention, a deliberate step to disassociate himself from the Griffiths legacy that had once defined him.

Richard had grown up under the shadow of Griffiths' name, a name that carried with it the weight of both pride and pain. Once associated with dignity and hard work in Worthenbury, it also reminded them of the struggles and tragedies that had haunted their lives.

For Richard, the decision to become Walters was a way to carve out his identity, free from the burden of his family's legacy. He had been acutely aware of the whispers and judgments that followed his family, mainly the rumours surrounding his mother's untimely death and the scandal that had tainted their name.

The final push came as he struggled to find his place in the world, particularly after the return to Liverpool after the death of his mother. With its opportunities and challenges, the city offered him a chance to start anew, to build a life on his own terms. But every time he introduced himself as Richard Griffiths, he felt a pang of discomfort, as if the name reminded him of a life that wasn't entirely his own. It wasn't just the past he wanted to escape—the expectations, the assumptions, and the inevitable comparisons to his prizefighter father and the family legacy.

So, he chose the name Walters, which carried no history, baggage, or connection to the past. The name felt right; it was simple, strong, and unburdened by the past.

By adopting the name Walters, Richard sought to redefine himself and forge a new path. He wanted to be known for his merits, decisions, and life rather than as a continuation of the Griffiths story.

As he stood overlooking the Mersey, Richard Walters felt a sense of peace. The brine-laden air mingled with the scent of tobacco from his clay pipe, a comforting reminder of simpler times amidst the weight of his thoughts. Dressed smartly despite the warm weather, Richard felt the mantle of responsibility settles upon him, a weight akin to balancing the world on his shoulders.

Coins bearing the likeness of the recently departed Queen Victoria jingled in his pocket, a constant reminder of the era he now lived in—a time of profound change and opportunity. His gaze drifted over the tall ships gliding in and out of the docks, vessels laden with exotic goods and passengers to distant lands. The Americas beckoned with promises of adventure and renewal, a dream Richard still considered for his growing family.

The cobbled streets below were alive with the sound of daily life—the clatter of horse-drawn carriages mingled with the sound of trams, bicycles, motorbikes and motor cars. Among these sounds, Richard's attention was drawn to a lone figure struggling up the street's steep incline. A boy, perhaps fifteen or so, was pushing a heavy-framed bicycle, his young face flushed from exertion. His straw boater was perched wearily on his head, and his clothes were smudged with the day's work at Green's the Butchers.

Richard smiled at the sight, recognising the lad as his half-brother, Joe Green. The boy had grown considerably, yet the traces of his youth were still evident in his gait and expression. Richard's smile widened as he approached, his eyes twinkling with mischief.

"Ah, young Joe!" Richard called out, his voice carrying a playful lilt. "What's that on your shirt, lad?"

Joe glanced down at his stained shirt, a weary grin tugging at the corners of his mouth. Before he could respond, Richard flicked his hat playfully, sending it tumbling to the ground. Joe chuckled, stooping to retrieve it and placing it back on his head with a resigned smile.

"Just a bit of this and that, Richard," Joe replied, his voice carrying the exhaustion of a long day. "Green's is a busy place."

Richard clapped Joe on the back with brotherly affection. "Come along, young Joseph. Let's wet the baby's head, shall we?"

Joe's eyes brightened at the suggestion, and he followed Richard with a sense of anticipation. They made their way to a nearby pub where the rich aroma of ale beckoned. Richard's playful grin remained as he guided Joe through the door.

Inside, the pub was a lively haven filled with the hum of conversation and the clinking of glasses. With his easy charm and unyielding confidence, Richard managed to persuade the bartender to serve them despite Joe's tender age. It was a small triumph but one that made Joe's tired face light up with gratitude.

"Here's to the new beginnings!" Richard declared, raising his glass in a toast. "To Albert Edward—your nephew."

Joe raised his glass with a nod, a mixture of pride and relief evident in his expression. The clinking of their glasses was accompanied by the warm murmur of approval from the other patrons, who seemed to sense the moment's significance.

As they drank, Richard leaned in close to Joe, his voice lowered to a conspiratorial whisper. "You know, lad, it's been a long road from Coventry to here. But seeing you grow up and make something of yourself makes all the hardships worthwhile."

Joe's gaze softened as he looked at Richard, his half-brother and guardian. "Thank you, Richard. For everything. It's about having someone believe in me."

Richard's smile was both tender and wistful. "We've all had our share of troubles, Joe. But family, well, family's what makes it all bearable."

The conversation drifted to lighter topics, and Joe found himself laughing. Richard's infectious enthusiasm and the camaraderie of the pub provided a welcome reprieve from the rigours of his daily toil.

As the evening drew to a close, the two made their way out of the pub, the cool night air a refreshing contrast to the warmth inside. Richard's thoughts turned to his own journey from his childhood to his new life in Liverpool. He had adopted the name Walters following his mother's passing, a deliberate choice to shed the shadow of his prizefighter father and create a fresh start for himself and his family. His wife, Alice, and their young son, Richard Jr., now bore the same surname, symbolising their collective new beginning. Joe had chosen Griffiths as his surname for reasons self-evident. Harry, too—in his new home with his half-sister Lizzy on Stoney Stanton Road, Coventry.

The losses of Richard and Alice's infant sons, John and William, years earlier had been a painful blow, yet Richard had found solace in the stability he could provide. Joe's presence in their home had been a testament to that resilience. Despite the circumstances of Joe's birth, Richard had embraced him almost as a son, and together, they had forged a bond that was both unbreakable and deeply meaningful.

As they walked home, Joe's thoughts turned to the future, and he found himself reflecting on his dreams and aspirations. Richard had always been a guiding force in his life, offering support and encouragement even when the path ahead seemed uncertain.

When they arrived back at the modest house on Catherine Street that they shared, Alice greeted them with a warm smile. The flickering light of the oil lamps cast a gentle glow over her features, and her eyes sparkled with a mix of affection and curiosity.

"How was the celebration?" she asked, her voice full of genuine interest.

"It was grand," Richard replied, his arm draped comfortably over Joe's shoulders. "We toasted Albert and had a good laugh. Joe's had a long day, but he's done well."

Alice's gaze softened as she looked at Joe. "You've worked hard, Joe. You deserve to enjoy a moment of respite."

Joe nodded, a smile of appreciation on his face. "Thank you, Alice. It's been a long road, but I'm grateful for all that's been offered."

The family settled into the cosy living room, where the warmth of the fire provided a comforting backdrop to their evening. Richard and Alice spoke of their plans for the future, their voices filled with a blend of optimism and practical consideration.

"We've been discussing the possibility of opening a shop one day," Richard said, his tone reflective. "If there's an opportunity to bring in business and perhaps offer Joe a prominent role in the business."

Alice nodded thoughtfully. Thuring to Joe she added, "It sounds like a wonderful idea. You've shown a remarkable commitment to your work, and it would be fitting to reward your dedication."

Joe's eyes widened with excitement at the prospect, and he found himself dreaming of a future where he could build on his grandfather's legacy. The idea of becoming a respected businessman, following in the footsteps of the man who had once been a cornerstone of Liverpool's culinary world, was a source of great pride.

As the night wore on, the family's conversation turned to the recent changes in their lives and the ways in which they had adapted to their new circumstances. Richard spoke of the challenges they had faced and the lessons they had learned; his words imbued with a sense of resilience and hope.

"We've all come a long way," he said, his voice carrying a note of determination. "And while the road has been fraught with difficulties, it's also been paved with moments of joy and accomplishment."

Alice reached out, placing a comforting hand on Richard's. "We've built something meaningful here, Richard. And with Joe's future looking brighter, I believe we're on the right path."

The conversation continued into the night, their words a blend of reflection and anticipation. The promise of new beginnings and the strength of their familial bonds provided a sense of assurance, guiding them through the uncertainties of the future.

Richard felt a deep sense of fulfilment as they prepared to retire for the evening. Trials and triumphs had marked the journey to Liverpool, but the family he had built and the life he had created were testaments to his enduring spirit.

In the quiet of the night, Richard stood by the window, gazing out at the city that had become his home. The soft glow of the street lamps cast a gentle light over the cobbled streets, and the distant murmur of the Mersey reminded him of the ever-present tides of change.

He knew that the path ahead would not always be smooth, but he faced it with a renewed sense of purpose. With his family by his side and the support of those he loved, Richard was ready to embrace whatever the future held, guided by the lessons of the past and the promise of a brighter tomorrow.

By 1901, the once-ambitious watchmaker Tom Green had descended into a life of hardship and obscurity. The years had not been kind to him, and the promise of a bright future in Coventry had long since faded into a distant memory. Tom had once dreamed of building a prosperous life, but as time passed, those dreams were steadily eroded by the harsh realities of life.

On 15 October 1898, Tom found himself on the wrong side of the law for a second time that year, charged with drunkenness and disorderly conduct. The local newspaper recounted the incident with cold detachment: Thomas Green, a watchmaker of no settled abode, was ordered to pay 5 shillings and 6 pence, along with 8 shillings in costs, or face seven days' imprisonment in default.

Unable to pay the fine, Tom served his time, another brief and sobering stint in jail that marked the culmination of his downward spiral.

By the turn of the century, Tom Green had become a pauper, residing in the Coventry Workhouse. Now sixty years old, the once-skilled watch motioner was listed as "retired," though the term seemed a cruel mockery of the reality he faced. With its stark walls and disciplined life, the workhouse was far from his youth's lively workshops and vibrant discussions. The man who had once talked of fortunes and prospects was now reduced to a forgotten figure, living out his days in the bleak institution that had become his final refuge.

Both of Tom's family had scattered, the bonds frayed by tragedy and time. His son, Joe, had moved to Liverpool, where he lived with his step-brother Richard, the son of the woman Tom had likely caused the death of in a fit of rage a few years earlier. The weight of that crime had hung over Tom's life like a dark cloud, and the knowledge that his son now lived with the victim's child added another layer of bitterness to his existence. Meanwhile, his other son, Harry, had remained in Coventry, where he lived with a half-sister. The family ties were complex and strained, shaped by the troubled past that Tom had never been able to escape. Though they lived apart, the echoes of Tom's life reverberated through their own, a reminder of the man he had once been and the broken path he had taken.

As 1901 drew to a close, Tom Green's life starkly contrasted with the promise it had once held. The bustling city of Coventry, with its thriving watchmaking industry, had moved on without him, and the dreams of prosperity and success were long gone.

© Ken Walters

Printed in Great Britain
by Amazon